D1440508

By Geoffrey Household

The Spanish Cave

The Third Hour

The Salvation of Pisco

Gabar and Other Stories

Rogue Male

Arabesque

The High Place

A Rough Shoot

A Time to Kill

Tales of Adventurers

Fellow Passenger

The Exploits of Xenophon

Against the Wind

The Brides of Solomon and
Other Stories

Watcher in the Shadows

Thing to Love

Olura

Sabres on the Sand

The Courtesy of Death

Prisoner of the Indies

Dance of the Dwarfs

Doom's Caravan

The Three Sentinels

The Lives and Times of
Bernardo Brown

Red Anger

The Cats to Come

Escape into Daylight

Hostage: London

The Last Two Weeks of
Georges Rivac

The Europe That Was

The Sending

Capricorn and Cancer

Summon the Bright Water

Rogue Justice

Arrows of Desire

The Days of Your Fathers

Face to the Sun

Born in Bristol in 1900 and educated at Magdalen College, Oxford, Geoffrey Household worked all over the world, including Eastern Europe, the USA, the Middle East and South America, as, among other things, a banker, a salesman and an encyclopaedia writer. He served in British intelligence in the Second World War. His other works include *A Rough Shoot*, *Watcher in the Shadows*, *Rogue Justice* and an autobiography, *Against the Wind*. He died in 1988.

A Rough Shoot

GEOFFREY HOUSEHOLD

An Orion paperback

First published in Great Britain in 1951
by Michael Joseph
This paperback edition published in 2013
by Orion Books,
an imprint of The Orion Publishing Group Ltd,
Carmelite House, 50 Victoria Embankment,
London EC4Y 0DZ

An Hachette UK company

3 5 7 9 10 8 6 4 2

A CIP catalogue record for this book
is available from the British Library.

ISBN 978-1-7802-2430-5

Typeset by Input Data Services Ltd, Bridgwater, Somerset

Printed and bound in Great Britain
by Clays Ltd, St Ives plc

The Orion Publishing Group's policy is to use papers that
are natural, renewable and recyclable products and
made from wood grown in sustainable forests. The logging
and manufacturing processes are expected to conform to
the environmental regulations of the country of origin.

www.orionbooks.co.uk

A Rough Shoot

IT ALL BEGAN on an autumn evening so silent and peaceful that no one who had the luck to be out-of-doors, with copse and downland stretching away from him till the folds of England vanished into a mist of grey and green, could have a thought of human violence. We had had two weeks of storm, and then came this Tuesday, October 18th, which belonged to late summer. All the life of grass and hedgerow was too busy satisfying hunger to be on guard. I didn't fire a shot the whole afternoon – not for lack of opportunity but because I wanted to see what game I had on the shoot and what were its movements if undisturbed.

I had rented very cheaply the rough shooting over 450 acres of a remote Dorset farm. The sport wouldn't have appealed to a man who liked driven pheasants or to a syndicate who expected the mixed bag to pay for their week-end. You had to work for your game. But on a favourable afternoon, if your liver and eyes were in good order – for it was speed that counted – you might come home with a brace of partridges, a hare, and of course all the rabbits you cared to kill. I shot purely for the pot, and anything I did not want I left for another day. I did not even use a dog. That will horrify the purist, but I would assure him that I seldom blazed away at the improbable, and that a bird which I couldn't retrieve myself was rare. Dull? Yes, if your fun is to fire off a lot of cartridges. No, if you shoot only for what the larder will hold. Of course with a dog I would have put up more pheasants from the hedgerows, but I got enough.

I only went up to the shoot on Saturday afternoons. Everybody knew that. Blossom, who was the tenant farmer, would have sworn to it, and I daresay that later he did. This Tuesday evening visit was due to accidents: that I had a slack afternoon at the office; that my gun happened to be at the gunsmith's, waiting to be picked up; and that the weather promised a glorious hour before the sudden autumn twilight.

I did not use my gun, and I moved around the shoot silently and for the most part under cover. I wanted to know the permanent population and its taste in feeding-grounds. A little before sunset I established myself in the thick boundary hedge, whence I had an excellent view of four other hedges and a long, warm slope of down.

Blossom's farm was long and narrow, running roughly north and south. Down the centre was the level, bare water-shed. The western slope was sharp, dropping to water meadows and a busy road; its short turf was dotted with clumps of thorn, gorse and bramble, so thick that even hounds were baffled and the foxes and rabbits kept up the balance of nature undisturbed. The eastern slope was slight, and fell away gradually to the boundary hedge which, in places, was a jungle twenty feet thick. To the south was a hilltop barn and outhouses, and beyond them a few primmer, kinder meadows.

I stayed on in the hedge till dusk, watching the movements of a flock of pigeons. There wasn't a soul about. Ploughing was over, and there would be little work on the slopes until the kale came to be cut for winter feed and the sheep were folded on the roots. That autumn the whole work of the farm was going on in the water meadows and in the fields beyond the barn.

At right-angles to the boundary hedge was another, which had thrown out great domes and bastions of bramble. I was astonished to see, appearing from the curve of one of these bushes, the seat of a generous pair of trousers. The man was apparently pegging something down just inside the hedge, and working backwards towards me. He half turned, and laid on the turf some sort of spike with a broad head.

Of course my mind leapt at once to rabbit traps; but when at last the man stood up, I saw that he wasn't a farm labourer, and wasn't dressed like a person who would be interested in rabbits. The expanse of cloth which he had persistently presented to me was town trouser.

If he were poaching, I thought, he ought to have either a dog or a companion. I looked more carefully into the dusk, and sure enough I found the companion. He was standing quite motionless on the top of the bank, under and against an ivy-covered oak, whence he could see for quarter of a mile on all sides of him. His disciplined stillness had its reward. A cock pheasant flew up to roost in the opposite tree. The trapper in the hedge saw it, drew an air pistol from his pocket, and shot it neatly down.

This made me unduly angry. I wouldn't have minded a bit if they had been local villagers out for next Sunday's dinner, but from their clothes I knew they were not. Somehow I got it into my head that they were commercial poachers, come all the way from London or Bournemouth to supply the black market. I didn't stop to think that, if they were, they wouldn't be working hedgerows but would clear out some big estate where one overworked gamekeeper still managed to keep up a stock of game.

The watcher on the bank looked down at the ping of the shot. He hardly spoke above a whisper, but gave the impression of being almost hysterical with petty annoyance. The man with the air pistol said something obviously rude, picked up the pheasant and returned to his job. He continued to work with his back to me, now well outside the bush but still presenting his broad and perfect target.

The temptation was too great. I didn't want the bother of handing them over to the law – supposing I could catch them – but I did want to teach them a lesson. The range was about eighty yards, far enough, I thought, to hurt, but to do no damage that a probe and a little disinfectant couldn't cure. I let him have a charge of No. 5 shot in the seat of the pants.

I talk lightly of this shocking brutality, but my conscience was and is appalled by the result. He straightened
himself with a jerk, completely off balance as if he were
diving from a springboard, and crashed heavily to the
ground. He kicked twice and lay still, his face and shoulders on the thorns of the blackberry bush. His companion
jumped down the far side of the bank and bolted across
country with no thought but for his own safety. I didn't
call to him to stop. I was paralysed by the shock of what
I had done. And there was little doubt of it. No man who
had life in him would lie in that position.

I don't know how long I stared at him, perhaps ten seconds, perhaps twenty – a stillness which was partly horror
and partly habit, acquired in war, of not giving my cover
away. Then I dashed out of the hedge, taking a smack over
the eye from an ash sapling, and ran to him.

I didn't move the body at first, fearing, impossible
though it seemed, that I had damaged the spine. I raised
his coat, cut the waistband of his trousers and tore them
down the seam. The pattern of the shot was regular and
very shallow, and exactly where it ought to have been. If
a beater, in the days of big shoots, had suffered such an
accident, he would have felt that a pint of beer and a brace
of pheasants amply repaid the inconvenience.

Then I turned him over, and understood. He was like
the men in the Bible. He had fallen on his sword. One of
the broad-headed spikes had been lying on the ground,
point uppermost like a giant thumb-tack, and the round,

5

shiny metal base was now pinned, a crimson-bordered decoration, to his left breast.

Instinctively I took hold to pull it out. Then a sort of panic reason took command and I let go, and wiped my fingerprints off it with his coat. Then I thought: *Oh Lord, they'll spot that somebody has wiped it!* And after that my imagination took me through an entire dialogue with the police.

That damned mark across my eye. Signs of a struggle. You shot at him. Then he struck you. You lost your temper and stabbed him. How did the dead man's clothes come to be torn? A wound of the spine, you thought! Ah, trying to make it manslaughter instead of murder, are you? Have you a respect for human life, Mr Taine? Yes, profound. In the war you won a D.C.M. as a corporal, I believe? Yes, I did. How many men did you kill on that occasion? Damn you, do you suppose I counted them? You had further decorations after you were commissioned? Yes, I did. You seem to have enjoyed this single-handed stuff? I hated it, but my chaps were about all in. Come, come, Mr Taine, now what really happened after the man struck you?

Well, no doubt I exaggerated. Perhaps some proofs could have been discovered by examination of the ground that my story was true. Perhaps I should never have been in the dock on a charge of murder. But most certainly I was guilty of manslaughter.

Now, if I am to explain properly the panic I was in, and what I did, I must tell a little about myself. My name is

Roger Taine. I am thirty-four, with a family and no capital. I have a good job as Dorset agent for a big quarry combine, producing cement, roofing tiles, special bricks, stone for building and gravel for roads, and all sorts of by-products that interest an up-to-date architect or county surveyor. What with commission and salary, I've no complaints; but my family, of course, has no security beyond my own earning power.

So, as I stood over the corpse and watched the dark shadow – in a dusk already too deep to distinguish colour – spreading over his clothes from beneath the head of that gigantic thumb-tack, I passed from the police interrogation to what the judge would say. Shooting a harmless poacher as if I were some callous county magnate a hundred and fifty years ago. At the best, criminally negligent. At the worst, a savage sadist from whom society must be protected. Make an example of him. Five years.

I couldn't expect to get less, and I deserved it. But when you have a family it's not so much the sentence which counts as the result of it – the complete, irrevocable breaking of the continuity between past and future. I'm not one of your go-getters. A small post as a clerk with some charitable firm would be all I could hope for – and there, for the rest of my life, I should remain.

After hearing the judge's remarks, I had no doubt at all that there weren't going to *be* any judge's remarks if I could help it. There was no one about. The dead man's companion had cleared out without ever seeing me or even knowing where the shot came from. I caught a glimpse of him bolting over the skyline towards a lonely road which ran across the downs some five hundred yards from Blossom's boundary, and then I saw the lights of a car gather speed and go tearing northwards.

I determined to get rid of the body where it wouldn't be found. It was, I admit, the act of a bad citizen, and, to my present way of thinking, a great deal worse than taking a careful shot – for I *was* careful – at that broad and unexpectedly vulnerable target from a perfectly safe range.

The disposal of bodies, as anyone knows who reads the Sunday papers, is not easy; sooner or later they turn up. I could not hope to find a permanent solution then and there. He was too heavy to carry far, and I had no spade. The most I could do was hide him, so that the man who ran away would assume, if he returned, that his companion had recovered and left. There was hardly any blood on the ground. No doubt police would have detected it, but it wasn't visible to a casual eye.

I strapped my game-bag over the wound and got him on my back. I was about to set off when it occurred to me that the traps were still in position. Was I to leave them or remove them? Either act might be evidence against me if there were any inquiry. I put him down, and hunted about in the last of the light. There were no traps at all. I found a spirit-level, a foot-rule, and three more of those murderous broad-headed spikes.

The sweat poured down my ribs. Had I shot at some

harmless Post Office surveyor? But that didn't make sense. The wildest conjectures went through my head. Commando training? Broadcasting engineers? Some kind of official experiment? I had hoped, with an irresponsible, cowardly optimism that I suspect is shared by every criminal, that there would only be the most perfunctory search for my supposed poacher, or none at all; his accomplice hadn't looked a man to get himself into the slightest trouble that could be avoided. But now it was absolutely certain that it would be some employer's duty to make the most exhaustive inquiries.

It is curious how every animal, even a quarry agent, is a creature of habit. In the midst of this blinding mess, which should have excluded all other worries, I found time to be upset at the thought of returning home too late. My wife knew that I was up at the shoot, for I had telephoned from Dorchester after leaving my office. She would be anxious when I didn't return at nightfall, and the children would catch her mood and refuse to go to sleep. I hated the thought of inventing some long and complicated lie. I never do lie to her. There's no reason for it.

That made me impatient, and over-anxious for a quick and temporary solution. I should have bicycled home, got out my car, and taken the body a hundred miles away from my shoot. The following night when, for all I knew, the place might be teeming with policemen, it would be impossible. The bicycle I must explain. Partly to save petrol, but more to keep fit, I always bicycled to and from the office on days when I knew I wasn't going to need the car. And so that evening the bicycle was all I had.

I carried my burden half a mile along the top of the down, and dropped it, together with all its tools, into a rabbit warren. This was a hollow which must once have been a dew-pond or a flint pit. The steep sides were honeycombed with rabbit holes, so large and so close together that once when I climbed down to pick up a shot rabbit the earth gave way and I sank over the knees. It was an unsavoury spot, with the carcasses of half a dozen sheep at the bottom, which had died of disease and been thrown there to rot.

I stamped on the tunnels and galleries until the soil caved in. Then I laid the corpse in this irregular trench and lightly covered it. In the pockets and on the clothes there was nothing to prove identity – or at any rate, nothing that I could see by the light of matches. I was careful to leave no smooth slope of new earth, and reckoned that there would be nothing suspicious to a casual eye. The only risk I ran was from a dog, which could track me across the down if he were put on to my scent in time.

I picked up my gun and returned to my bicycle, which was leaning against a haystack just off the upper road. On the way home I stopped at the edge of a fast stream and let the water run over my game-bag and my coat to dissolve the blood. I wished to heaven that I had had more experience of police methods than odd bits and pieces gathered from newspaper reports and detective stories.

War experience – well, there was that, and I suppose in a way it was useful. At any rate, I had carried a dead man before, though I didn't know he was dead till we arrived. War, too, had convinced me that a remarkable deal of crime is never discovered at all.

It was nine o'clock when I got home, and, as I expected, Cecily was very worried. She had visions of a shooting accident; they were not unreasonable, and, if you think of it, they were correct. My lateness was inexplicable. If I had stopped at a pub or to see a friend on my way home, I should have telephoned. She knew, too, that I wouldn't willingly disappoint our two boys, who had been promised a long story before bedtime.

I told her that I had stayed very late looking for a dead bird, and that on the way back a tyre had been punctured (which was true, for I had driven a pin into it just before reaching home), so I had had to walk. She gave me a silent, doubtful look once or twice in the evening, which meant that she knew there was trouble on my mind, and that she was too proud to ask for it. I pretended to be sulky just because I hadn't shot anything.

The next day I awoke – if it can be called waking after such a night – with an atrocious, evil conscience. To prepare the way for my absence, I told Cecily that I intended to do a round of customers and prospects, and that, as I was going to be in the north of the county, I should call on my opposite number in Salisbury and stay the night. This was a perfectly normal routine; nevertheless she asked me diffidently to call her from Salisbury just to say that I was all right. I tied my bicycle to the roof of the car – on the grounds that I couldn't be bothered to mend the puncture myself – and surreptitiously threw a spade into the back.

I told my clerk – there were only the two of us in the office – that I was going to do a round of visits, and that I shouldn't come back. Then I drove twice round the shoot through all the lanes and roads that were near to it. There was no sign at all of anything wrong, no cars of police or strangers parked by the roadside or on the cart tracks.

I dropped in on old Blossom, the farmer from whom I rented the shooting. We had a mug of cider together – he was one of the few men left in the county who still made his own – and talked of local affairs. He evidently hadn't been disturbed by police or anyone else. He mightn't have told me, of course, if he had; but I knew him well enough to recognize his manner when he was being heavily discreet. You could always hear him turning on the caution, and forcing his geniality a bit.

As drove out of Blossom's gate and over the stream, I passed a man standing on the roadside near the bridge. He looked brisk and important, like a fussy foreman on a job he didn't understand. In the ordinary way he would never have made me suspicious. Blossom's farm, the tall elms and the clear chalk stream made a pretty, if somewhat obvious picture that always attracted the holiday-making townsman. It was a bit late, however, for holidays, and it wasn't a week-end; and then the man was dressed as some minor, pestiferous government employee, yet had no vehicle in sight. I drove very slowly away, and watched him in the mirror. He was looking after my car; he wrote something, presumably its number, in a notebook.

I pulled up a little farther on and climbed a slope to observe him. He seemed to be making a sort of census of traffic. The vet and the baker both stopped at the farm, and, as if glad of the opportunity, he asked them questions. His self-satisfaction was obvious, even from a distance.

I couldn't believe this little man was a policeman, or that his questions were police routine. If anyone had approached the Dorset Constabulary with some story, necessarily vague, of a man shot on Blossom's land, their very first move would be to interview Blossom and inspect the ground. They wouldn't put a plain-clothes detective on the job before they knew whether there was a word of truth in the yarn.

Somebody else, however, seemed to have acted quickly. My thoughts returned to the imagined gang of game and poultry thieves. Perhaps they had some ingenious method of attracting things wild and edible by light or by some device that needed careful levelling. In any case, this was a warning that some sort of investigation was going on. My simple plan had to be scrapped. I couldn't risk leaving my car anywhere near the shoot, under possible observation, while I dug up the body and carried it.

I drove on and lunched very late at a remote pub overlooking the Blackmoor Vale, where the landlord, who was a friend of mine, always had something solid to eat which food controllers had never heard of. On this occasion it was a badger ham, and very good it was. I was amazed at my appetite, and ashamed – but then I realized that my mind, all unknown to me, had been making deductions. Somebody was as yet unwilling to call in the police; and that could only mean that my shot was – well, not justified from any legal or moral point of view, but at least the sort of accident that did occur in the world to which the dead man had belonged. The instancy of his companion's escape bore it out. Why run, unless he had a very guilty conscience or had been prepared to be shot at? Any normal citizen, however timid, would have protested then and there (though keeping perhaps carefully under cover) and would have gone to the police that very night.

So my conscience was easier, and my appetite made me realize it. I wasn't quite in the position of a drunken driver who kills a man on the road and hides the body. I was more like the householder who shoots at a burglar and accidentally kills him. The law would take a serious view of such a crime, but the householder himself would not; and, if he could easily get rid of the body, he might be fool enough, as I was, to try.

I was strongly tempted to leave well alone; but then I should be at the mercy of the merest accident all through the winter – Blossom's inquisitive sheep-dogs, the rain or the rabbits themselves. No, the body couldn't be left where it was. On the other hand, it could no longer be removed by road. The only solution was to find a better hiding-place on the shoot itself.

That wasn't going to be easy. Hedges and coverts were thick with all the dying vegetation of summer, and I couldn't dig in such stuff – apart from the physical difficulty of it – without leaving a patch of beaten ground which would be conspicuous to any determined searcher. Digging in the open and levelling off so that nothing suspicious remained was, at any rate at night, quite impossible. At last, in my after-lunch meditation, it occured to me that I needn't do either.

In the north-east corner of the shoot, at the top of the boundary hedge, was a tumble-down piece of dry-stone walling which had once surrounded a barn or cottage, and now contained only a clump of beeches and a jungle of brambles. On the south side, just off Blossom's land, was a field which had been freshly ploughed and harrowed. I intended to pull down a short stretch of wall, dig a shallow hole and replace the stones when I had finished. The earth could be scattered on the new-turned earth of the field, and raked over with a branch. The nettles and bramble on the inner side of the wall would be undisturbed, and, if the job were neatly done, the two persons most concerned could rest in peace.

In the afternoon I drove back along the upper road and still saw nothing to disquiet me. I stopped for an instant to hide the spade in a ditch where I could pick it up later. When I reached Dorchester I put my car in the public car park and collected my bicycle at the little shop which had mended the puncture. I kept to the back streets, for I didn't want to run into Cecily, who might be in town, or any of my friends.

After dusk I approached the shoot, very cautiously and without lights, along the upper road. I was prepared to give up the whole plan if I passed a single stranger, but I did not. For three miles, without either village or cottage, this narrow, well-metalled by-road switchbacked up and down across the high ground. There were several ways of scrambling across country from the road to Blossom's land, but only one regular track – if you can call a couple of ruts in the grass a track.

I carefully reconnoitred the point where the track met the road. The man who ran away had taken this route the previous night. By bending close to the ground I could just make out the print of tyres in the mud where his car had been parked. Then I rode on up the road, recovered the spade, hid my bicycle, and worked my way silently across the fields to the clump of beeches and the wall. There I was fairly close to the pit, but a good half mile from the corner of the hedge where the accident had happened.

It was a gusty night, with thin clouds whose lower edge occasionally touched the top of the downs and enveloped them in mist. The trees within the wall creaked and whispered, and the thorn and holly and elder of the great hedge rattled their branches and dying leaves. There was enough noise to cover any that I might make myself. Even so, before I started to remove the stones I sat still and watched and listened. The clouds were often tenuous enough to show the shape of a half moon, and then I could see a hundred yards into the milky and uneasy world that surrounded me.

One by one I removed the flat stones of the wall, placing them on the bare earth of the field so that I would know in what order they went back. I hadn't of course taken on the impossible task of replacing a neat wall in position. I wanted only to leave the tumble of stones, the wall-shaped object, looking much as it had before. While I worked I had my back towards the length of the boundary hedge, and I can't say I liked it. With my back unguarded, with such a beastly task in front of me, and in not too deep a darkness, across which flitted the wisps and wraiths of cloud, I had to keep a tight hold on imagination.

I kept too tight a hold. Any balance was impossible. Either I had to investigate every cracking branch, every inexplicable sound, or none at all. And so it was that I didn't pay attention until the final rush of feet.

I ascribe my safety to sheer animal panic, for I am no athlete. All my suppressed fears exploded instantaneously and I jumped sideways and off, like a hare out of her form. As my pursuers stumbled over the stones, I increased a lead of five yards to twenty. I led them towards the road and then dived – literally dived, head first – over a gap in the hedge which I knew was closed by five strands of barbed wire. They crashed into it as I picked myself up, and gave tongue loudly in oaths that certainly weren't those of local men. There were two of them. One had a cultured accent, and a loud and hearty voice. The other was a foreigner. Their speed and energy made me certain that neither was the man I had seen at Blossom's gate. Dense cloud was moving over the ground, and in that foggy darkness I could get no impression at all of height or build. It was a comforting thought that to them too I must have been nothing but a piece of night which moved.

By the time they got clear of the wire and were able to listen to anything but themselves, I was safe. I dropped to the ground and waited. One of them produced a torch that he hadn't had time to use before, and flashed it half-heartedly around. I noticed that he held it away from him at the full stretch of his arm. It was obvious that he thought I might fire at the light. This was a cheering reminder that I was not dealing with police, and that my pursuers, whoever they were, expected a more formidable enemy than an innocent and hitherto respectable salesman.

They gave up the search for me and returned to the wall. There of course they found my spade and walked off with it. That was a disaster. There would be some wonderful sets of my finger-prints on that spade. The Englishman said to the other:

'Hold it by the blade, man!'

So that was that, and the end of me if ever they chose to go to the police. I could never produce any convincing story to explain what I was doing with a spade in that corner of the shoot.

They walked away diagonally across the fields, aiming – I had to gamble on it – for the cart track. As soon as I was sure, I ran straight to my bicycle, tore silently up the road and reached the junction a little before them. They had no waiting car. They turned left and walked along the stretch of road I had just covered, one of them carrying the spade over his shoulder and still holding it by the blade. I followed, trailing them by the sound of their footsteps.

When they got over the brow of the hill I decided to take a chance. The road was good and my cycle well oiled. It made no more noise than dead leaves blowing over the tarmac. They were talking together as I swept down behind them and when they heard me it was too late. I passed them at about fifteen miles an hour, swerved, grabbed at the spade and wobbled twice across the road – but I had it, and the torch was flashed too late. I heard them begin to run, and I put on speed.

Further on I came to a motorcycle and sidecar, parked just off the road without lights. I don't suppose anyone else would have noticed it, but I was looking for their transport, and I knew all the gates and gaps where it could be. I had about a couple of minutes to deal with it. I caught carburettor and petrol pipe a devastating swipe with the spade, wrenched off the clutch cable, and then saw a handy billet of wood with which I wrecked the spokes of the back wheel. I lost my temper with that motorcycle, and I left it looking as if I had. Then I rode peacefully back to Dorchester, recovered my car, and was home before midnight with a story that I hadn't had to stay the night in Salisbury after all.

It is now time to say something of my silent Cecily. She seldom says what she thinks. On the other hand, unless she is talking to fools who expect it of her, she never says what she doesn't think. This apparent quiescence – a reluctance, one might call it, to disturb the status quo – makes her very easy to live with: too easy, perhaps, for I am inclined to accept her longer silences without inquiring into the cause so closely as I ought.

Such masculine laziness was now useful. I could pretend I didn't notice her mood. She, on her part, was much too proud to ask me the reason for my odd behaviour two nights running. I don't want to give the impression that I had to explain all my movements to her. Of course I didn't. I was a hardworking quarry agent, frequently on the road at short notice. No, I mean that ours was as good a marriage as you could find. If I were anxious or excited, she always knew it; if it were she who went through some silent crisis, I usually knew it. But we were both quite capable of feigning to see nothing wrong until the cloud over the other, whatever it was, had passed.

This peace which she created in our home helped me through the next forty-eight hours. When Cecily found a report in Thursday's evening paper of an abandoned motorcycle on the upper road, which had had its number plates removed and seemed to have been in a smash, I was able to grunt and answer, with complete lack of interest, that I supposed it was stolen. I wanted, of course, day and night, to go up to the shoot and see that the rabbits in their pits were undisturbed, but somehow I managed to control myself until the week-end.

On Saturday I took a full day off and went over the ground with a determined unconcern calculated to deceive any watcher. The knowledge that I might be in the field of somebody's glasses made me concentrate very nervously on my shooting – with the odd result that I couldn't miss.

I was careful not to go straight to the pit. When at last I did go there, in the normal course of walking the length of the down for a hare, the slope looked so natural that I wondered at my fears. Then I remembered that there were only nine inches of earth between me and discovery, and I thought of the cowardliness of my act and the cruelty of this lonely death. Yet it was certain that powerful friends knew of his death or disappearance, and would do whatever had to be done.

The stones from the wall were on the ploughed field where I had left them. I don't know what the next-door farmer, to whom this field belonged, made of them. Possibly he assumed that Blossom, with whom he was on very neutral terms, had needed some stones for walling and would clean up the mess in due season. Which of them owned this worthless little plot, with its trees and ruins and nettles, I never found out.

I sat down and ate my sandwiches at the top of the shoot, and as I let my eyes wander over the loved, familiar rise and fall of the land, I became aware that there was a question to be put to it. Those two men who nearly caught me – what were they doing in the north-east corner of the shoot? There was no reason why they should look for me at that end of the boundary hedge, and I was sure I hadn't made enough noise to attract them. Then suppose that they were not looking for me at all – had given it up – and were on their way back to the road. On their way back from what?

I found enough of their tracks to prove that they had come from the west, along a cattle-proof hedge that divided Blossom's down. Beyond it, the down ran on in a great expanse of close rabbit-turf which had never been ploughed. Close to the hedge were dense, rounded thickets of bramble that looked like the huts of a kaffir kraal. They repeated so exactly those domes and bastions where the dead man had been at work, that I wondered if the same mysterious activity might not have been carried on.

On my way home I felt, with a vague soldier's instinct, that the clue to the action must be found in the lie of the land. Yet never was there a more innocent patch of geography. Before me, to the south, was a great semi-circle of rolling country, ending in the coastal hills. The smooth hog's back where I was gave no impression of height and rose so gradually that it was not conspicuous or in any way a landmark; it was merely the highest point, level, spacious and remote, in a green bowl of farms and villages.

A week passed and nothing happened. I could almost accept an unexpected ring at the door-bell with equanimity. At any rate, I had no longer to force myself into unnatural calm. The weather was vile. There were two days of gales with torrents of rain, and then a thick fog came up from the Channel. This suited me well. I went on foot to the pit, not even risking a bicycle in case it should be seen and recognized, and created the appearance of a landslip which had dragged a thorn tree loose from its roots. Thereafter the spot was covered by enough earth and tangled vegetation to discourage man or dog.

The following Saturday afternoon I went out again with my gun, and came on old Blossom and one of his men carting hay from a stack in the southern meadows. He called me over when I shouted a good afternoon, and on the other side of the cart I found his landlord, Robert Heyne-Hassingham. Blossom introduced me as the man who had taken his shooting, and Heyne-Hassingham at once turned on the charm.

He had plenty of it, part hereditary and part acquired as a practising politician. He was an excellent landlord and a man of considerable influence in the county – indeed, in all the west of England. During the war he had been chosen, it was said, as the underground leader for a very wide area in the event of a successful German invasion.

After the war, however, he become a slightly comic figure to the average stolid citizen, for he began to take politics as seriously as any ardent socialist. He founded the People's Union, which had a lot of publicity till the newspapers grew tired of it. It was a sort of Boy's Brigade for grown-ups, full of Ideals, Service and Religion. Any religion would do. It appealed to disgruntled ex-servicemen, and was supposed to have a following among regular officers of the Army and Navy – a threat that we hadn't known since Cromwell's day. To the plain Englishman, however, who keeps his Ideals, Service and Religion packed away in the gun-room, well oiled and ready for use but emphatically out of reach of the children, the People's Union was offensive. It had a somewhat fascist smell of hierarchy. It paid lip-service to democracy, of course, but there was no doubt that if Heyne-Hassingham and his choirboys ever came to power – which no one thought remotely possible but themselves – Parliament would be even more of a rubber stamp than it is.

As I say, he turned on the charm, and naturally enough I was flattered and began to think – as one usually does on meeting an eminent public man in the flesh – that I had greatly misjudged him. He discussed gun and game, talked of old days when his father and the gamekeepers had brought up thousands of pheasants by hand, and asked me if I thought the pheasant was establishing itself successfully as a purely wild bird. I had no doubt that it was.

He knew his countryside, though I had the impression that he was entertaining me with what he had heard rather than what he had observed. That thin, rather ascetic face didn't really belong to our wealth of slow life.

'Your grandfather was a great friend of our family, Colonel Taine,' he said.

'Mr Taine,' I corrected him.

Inverted snobbery, I suppose. But it's ridiculous for an ordinary businessman to go walking about as a colonel.

'I was only thinking,' he smiled, 'how proud the old boy would have been of a grandson who commanded his battalion and collected all your gongs on the way.'

I didn't believe that my grandfather had any connection with the Heyne-Hassinghams – except that he sold them a famous ram of his own breeding – but I accepted this lush suggestion of friendship. Grandfather, if he visited their house at all, would certainly have made some memorable inroads on the Heyne-Hassingham cellar before parting with his ram.

'The country needs men like you,' he said.

That was an invitation, but I wasn't having any.

'We *are* a bit short of plain, contented chaps,' I answered.

'That is you?'

'It is.'

'You're rare then, and you're very lucky,' he said. 'But, believe me, in too many other cases content grows into self-satisfaction.'

He asked us both to stroll as far as his car with him, playing the busy man who did not want to part from agreeable company, but had to account for every minute of his time. His conversation was now mostly with Blossom, and about the high down. In answer to his questions Blossom, I remember, told him that the growth of the grass had been disappointing that dry summer, and that he wasn't putting any cattle or sheep on the down till the spring.

The car had been left on the upper road, so we passed that fatal angle of the boundary hedge. It was exactly as I and the dead man had left it, except that rain had cleared away the blood, if there ever was any, and restored the grass.

'By the way, Mr Blossom,' Heyne-Hassingham asked, 'have you agreed with your neighbour to leave that gap open, or is there a right of way?'

'Always bin open, an we keeps 'un open,' Blossom replied non-committally.

Heyne-Hassingham asked if strangers ever wandered through that way, and was told they didn't. Then his attention seemed to be drawn by the swarms of rabbits, and he wanted to know if Blossom sold the trapping. Blossom did. All game above ground was mine, but a professional trapper paid a useful sum for the right to take game below ground. He usually spent four or five nights after Christmas clearing out the big warrens.

Heyne-Hassingham kept on with his cross-examination. He stayed in character as an interested landlord, but was persistent as any lawyer.

'Is there any illicit trapping by local bad lads?' he asked.

'Not if Mr Taine don't. 'E should lam, 'e should! Bit o' wire and 'is old breeches, that's all 'e needs. Comes cheaper than bangin' off fourpence!'

Blossom chuckled and puffled under his scarves and waistcoats, and gave me an enormous wink to assure me he wasn't to be taken seriously.

'Up here often at night?' Heyne-Hassingham inquired, as if carrying on the joke.

'I? Never.'

This conversation made me uneasy. It might be innocent, but it was near enough to the bone to put me on my guard. And that was as well, for, when we came to the car, there was the handsome, nervous face which I had last seen staring, for a split second, at the dead companion in the bramble bush.

The man was leaning against Heyne-Hassingham's car with a rather too conscious grace. He was in his early forties, lean, hard and able. I think that even then I spotted him as the type of staff officer whom one most dislikes but from whom one cannot withhold respect. Heyne-Hassingham introduced him as Colonel Hiart.

'This is Mr Taine,' he said, 'who rents the shooting up here.'

There was a hardly perceptible note of mischief in his voice as he gave me my civilian title. He guessed just what I was going to think of Hiart, and let me know – if I were clever enough to see it – that the contrast between us amused him. He was a subtle and likeable creature.

Natural enough, I suppose. If he hadn't been, he could never have founded and held the devotion of his People's Union.

Hiart shook hands. His narrow, dark eyes were laid on me as directly and expressionlessly as the guns of a tank.

'Do you shoot?' I asked him.

'I fear,' he said, 'that I find it noisy and unnecessary.'

'I'd find it unnecessary too,' I retorted, 'if I still had army rations. But I must admit I enjoy it. I'll also admit that I think I ought not to.'

That was a perfectly sincere remark. I wasn't acting. Afterwards, when I knew a little more of Hiart, I saw that I couldn't have answered better. He had intended deliberately to provoke some reaction, probably brutal, which would give him a line on my character. I wouldn't like to say what he made of the reaction that in fact he got, but he must have thought it unlikely that I was a man to shoot strangers and remove their bodies.

When the car had driven away and Blossom had returned to his hay-carting, I started to tramp through the roots for partridge. It was merely to put up a show of activity. The coveys were far too wild at the end of October to be walked up.

I was perplexed, and in the blackest depression. There wasn't a shadow of doubt that Heyne-Hassingham and his tame colonel had come over to Blossom's farm on a Saturday afternoon in the hope of finding me, that they considered me a possible suspect, or, alternatively, a possible ally. All the tripe Heyne-Hassingham had talked about my grandfather's friendship for his family seemed to indicate that he wanted my own.

Ally in what? That I couldn't answer. I was shocked and alarmed to discover that Heyne-Hassingham, prominent, patriotic, and above suspicion, was connected with the runaway Hiart, with the violence of that nocturnal attempt on me, with a motorcycle so compromising that it had to be left abandoned and unclaimed.

I pulled myself together by remembering that only a week before I had expected every hour to be hauled in by the police for questioning. Well, that hadn't happened, and seemed unlikely to happen; but I began to think I would prefer the police to this fog of uncertainty. I didn't know whom to protect myself against. I even wondered whether I had interfered by my mysterious, unaccountable shot with some private action of the intelligence services. That, if it were so, made my guilt a thousand times worse.

When I got home there was further evidence that somebody was interested in my movements.

'Have you got a cigarette case that doesn't belong to you?' Cecily asked.

'No. Why?'

She said that a man had called up and wanted to know if I had found his case. She replied that I hadn't told her anything, and asked him where he had lost it. When he dined with me the week before last, he said, and added:

'Let's see. When was that?'

Now, this is a cautionary story for children on the virtue of never having secrets from one's wife. Cecily knew perfectly well that if I had dined with anyone at all, I should have come home full of it.

'Wednesday, of course,' he said.

That disastrous Wednesday, October 19th, when I had ostensibly been in Salisbury, was the only day I could have dined out. Any other wife, piqued at the fact that my doings had been exceptional and puzzling, would have eagerly swallowed the bait; but Cecily smelt something wrong with it.

'No,' she had answered instinctively. 'The only night he was out was Saturday.'

She saw the relief in my face. It may be that she even heard a gasp of tension freed. By sheer good sense she had ruled me out as a possible suspect.

'Darling,' she asked anxiously, 'you haven't ... ?'

'Yes? What?'

'Well, done anything against the law. But it's impossible!'

I avoided the direct answer.

'He *was* trying to find out if I came home late that night,' I said.

I told her, on the spur of the moment and very unconvincingly, that I was investigating a racket in building materials for my firm, and trying to get evidence that the police could not. She accepted it, but she knew very well that I would have told her that much long before, even if I didn't give the details. And she knew that I knew. There was nothing whatever hidden from either of us, except a bit of prosaic fact.

Cecily went upstairs to put the children to bed, and I gave myself a stiff gin. It did so much good that I had two more. The evening story turned out to be rather more imaginative than usual.

I was always allowed a wild twenty minutes with the children after their bath and before they were finally tucked up. This period was spent in some romp or other – suppressed by Cecily if it promised to be too exciting for sleep – or in stories. My two sons, Jerry aged seven and George aged five, had a taste, which I tried to satisfy, for improbabilities. Not fairies, but something near the shaggy dog story was what they liked. That night I started one about a nest of ants in the garden. When petrol was poured down the hole to destroy them, out they all came, saying thank-you-very-much and driving a communal car.

Cecily listened to the end of the story, and then we had supper in rather less silence than had been the custom for the last ten days. I warned her that if anyone seemed anxious to find out where I had been after dusk on the 18th and up to midnight on the 19th, she was to remember that I had been at home. And – as these people seemed clever at misusing the telephone – I suggested a code for our personal service. If I myself were on the telephone and I carried on with the ant story for the children, it meant that I was on this secret job and she must be wary.

Anyone purporting to give her a message from me would also mention ants.

It was no good to worry, no good to break in any way from my routine. Routine is a powerful drug, helping a sufferer to live on condition that he accepts a slightly deadened existence. So I worked hard and regularly during the week, and took my Saturday afternoon as usual on the shoot. It was the fifth of November, two and a half weeks from the death of the unknown.

The warren was still undisturbed. So, apparently, were my nerves, for I shot a hare almost on the edge of the pit. Then I walked back the length of the down, getting nothing at all on the way, towards the stacks and richer fields at the southern end of the farm.

I was just turning into the track which led past the barn and down to the valley, when, some way ahead of me and on the other side of a gate, I saw a small, tweedy, sporty-looking man earnestly watching the long grass in front of him.

'Hi, you!' he shouted. 'Stay just where you are!'

'Why?'

'Wait and see!'

He accompanied this order with a cheerful wave of his stick, and made gestures with his free hand in the direction of the field. He doubled round the angle of the hedge and disappeared.

His commanding voice had sounded thoroughly friendly, so I obeyed. Then I saw him crash through one of Blossom's neatest fences, as if he had had a horse between his legs, and up got the partridges. He was astonishingly right in his judgement. They skimmed across my front into the turnips, and I got a quick right and left which must have looked quite showy from where he was standing.

'Thank you,' I said when he came up. 'How on earth did you know what they'd do on strange ground?'

'Brought up with 'em,' he answered. 'Liked 'em for breakfast. One for me, brace for father.'

He was a fiery-looking little bouncer, about five and a half feet high with a pointed face and a thin sandy moustache. There was a network of scars on one side of his chin, and he had a slight limp which suggested still another war wound. His age was unguessable – somewhere between forty and fifty-five. Whatever it was, he was undoubtedly fighting fit, and his movements were fast and jerky as those of a well-strung puppet.

We had a short conversation – one of those curious interchanges wherein nothing whatever is revealed but instant mutual sympathy. I found myself saying:

'I can't offer you much sport, but if it would amuse you to join me up here any week-end, I'd be delighted.'

It was a wildly impulsive offer, especially as I had every reason to be suspicious of strangers. But he was so obviously a man from whom I could learn.

'No good!' he replied. 'Right eye gone. Pop in – pop out. Marble! Ever seen one?'

He handed me his right eye, and I bowed to it. I couldn't think of anything else to do.

'Try a left-hand gun,' I suggested.

'Yes. Some day. But no time since the war. Where did you learn to shoot?'

'I'm a farmer's son.'

'And what do you do now?'

'Sell stone.'

'Tombstones, ha?' he exploded joyfully. 'But you look like a soldier.'

'Well, I've been that too.'

'What rank?'

'Lieutenant-Colonel of sorts.'

'Didn't I say so? Once a colonel, always a colonel,' he decreed. 'Commanded your battalion?'

'As a matter of fact, I did.'

'Staff jobs, too?'

'Never!'

'Decorations?'

'Damn you, what business is it of yours?' I retorted. 'Who the hell are you?'

'Me? A murderer.'

I thought I had got him placed at last. The Dorset Mental Hospital wasn't far away, and they used to let out the less eccentric inmates for quiet country walks.

'First or second?' I asked.

'Eh? First, of course! Who wants to be a second murderer?'

'All the risk and none of the fun,' I agreed soothingly. 'What did you do to your victim?'

'Shot him. Shot him in the back right here somewhere.'

'Why?'

'That's just what I don't know. I've been looking for a chap like you to tell me.'

'What do you want me to tell you?'

'Why I am supposed to have killed a man hereabouts,' he answered, staring me straight in the eyes with a flash of the sanest and grimmest humour I ever saw.

So he wasn't a lunatic. So he knew that someone had met his death on my shoot. Was he a detective, or one of Heyne-Hassingham's people? How much did he know, and how did he know anything at all? Was it true that he himself had been accused of firing the shot?

It was impossible to answer any of those questions, so I tried to keep my face in its same casual and friendly expression, and play for time. I decided to carry on in his own chosen atmosphere of eccentricity.

'Who was he?' I asked.

'I don't know. There's a lot of people I'd shoot on sight. Back or front, ha! Which of them was this?'

'But *did* you kill him?'

'No. Did you?'

'Do I look as if I'd shoot a man in the back?' I replied with all the indignation I could pretend.

'Yes. Don't be a hypocrite! Never shot a German in the back? Must happen. Law of averages. Sometimes they're coming. Sometimes they're going. Colonel, I have watched the face of every man who visits this hill-top. You are the only one who would stick at nothing, and whose aim I'd trust – and, if I may say so, whom I'd trust myself.'

'Shall we tell your story to the police?' I asked.

'Think they'd understand it, do you, ha? I don't!'

'Will you tell it to me, then?'

'Certainly. Let us sit down.'

'Not here,' I said.

'Why? Wind too cold, or—?'

'Or,' I answered, taking the gamble.

I led him through the gate and over on to the steep western slope of the down. A narrow sheep path twisted into the heart of one of the clumps of furze, and opened out on to a patch of turf the size of a small room. There we were safe from observation, and overlooked the lower road that wound along the stream, past Blossom's farm, from village to village.

'Who are you?' I asked again.

'To hell with it!' he answered as if taking a sudden decision. 'General-of-Cavalry Peter Sandorski of the Polish Army.'

'You're in one of these resettlement camps?'

'Resettle my backside!' he replied.

'I was only wondering where you picked up English,' I explained.

'English governess.'

'She must have been an exceptional woman.'

'We had English grooms, too. Pay your penny and take your choice.'

'Whom did you fight for?'

'Poland,' he answered drily.

'I meant – with what army after the defeat?'

'The partition,' he corrected me. 'Oh, first the Russians, then the Germans. No other way of killing both, was there?'

'And you live in England?'

'Under the sky, my sympathetic colonel. Under the sky.'

Then he told me as much of his story as he thought fit for me to hear. I don't know how many secret organizations he served when it suited him – indeed, I doubt if he knew himself – but one was his own, formed by him and led by him. This private intelligence unit of his had picked up in the western zone of Germany an S.S. man with whom they had a seven-year-old account to settle.

Now, the real reason why Sandorski's people – who, he insisted, were plain non-party Polish officers and good Europeans – had kidnapped this brute was punishment, revenge, whatever you like to call it; and in due season they quietly dropped his weighted body into the Danube.

'I am a Pole, not a judge at Nuremberg,' Sandorski said to me sharply, noticing my shocked and – now I come to think of it – hypocritical expression.

Before they disposed of him, however, they interrogated him. He talked quite freely. Being a foolish and senti-mental German, he didn't think anybody would bother to kidnap and punish him for crimes he had committed seven years earlier. He assumed that these freelance Poles had picked him up because they wanted to question him about his recent doings, and he was ready enough to answer. He probably hoped they might employ him as a professional thug. And so he confessed a story that no one had ever suspected. He had just returned, he said, from England.

What had he been up to there? He had been flown over, he replied, for a special job, landing he didn't know where; nor did he know – for plans had been changed – what the job was to be. Immediately after his arrival he had been given a temporary assignment – and that was to catch Sandorski with the body of a man he had murdered the previous night.

The S.S. man was asked who told him that the killer was Sandorski. He replied that the dead man had had a companion, who escaped, and that the companion had said it was Sandorski. He didn't know the names of either the dead man or his companion.

From whom, then, did he take his orders, the interrogator asked. From an Englishman, he replied, with the cover name of Pink. A former naval officer, he believed. Pink was his contact, and Pink and he had gone out together to discover what Sandorski had been doing, and to catch him if they got a chance.

Had they seen him? Yes, and chased him. But Pink had been very doubtful if it was Sandorski at all. They had only got a glimpse of his back, once bent down as he ran and once leaning over the handlebars of a bicycle. He had wrecked their motorbike and sidecar, and vanished.

'Now then,' said Peter Sandorski, cutting short his narrative, 'I have friends everywhere. Even in your British intelligence services, when I behave myself. I asked them where, on the 19th October, a motorcycle was abandoned. No driver. No claim. The answer was precise. Of military exactitude, with a map reference. So here I am. I have watched. I have listened. I think I have identified the wall which was being pulled down when Pink and his late friend interrupted the person they thought was me. Colonel, if you could tell me whom I am supposed to have killed, you would do a service to your country. I tell you that' – he jumped up among the furze bushes and stood to attention – 'on my honour as an officer.'

I had no intention of confessing to him that I myself was the killer; nor, I think, did he then suspect it. He had been silently watching and weighing all the local people who could conceivably be mixed up in any sort of violent action, and had quite rightly assumed that I was the only one. Thereupon he had at once found – or forced, rather – a common sympathy.

I determined to measure out the information I would give. I had nothing to go on but liking and disapproval of him. This gallant little eccentric seemed to have a disregard for human life that was two hundred years out of date. But it could have been worse. He might have had a wholly modern disregard.

'Age about forty,' I said. 'Solid build and especially broad across the hips. Dressed in a wind-breaker and tweed trousers. I can't tell you much about his colouring.'

'Height?' he asked.

'Medium. About an inch taller than you.'

'That is tall,' he insisted severely. 'Nose? Chin?'

'Nose, nothing in particular. Jaw, square.'

'Can I have a look at him?'

'No.'

'Dig him up,' he suggested.

'How should I know where he is?'

'Mention of a spade. Who grabbed it on the road?'

'You did. And Pink will swear to it in court if it suits him.'

'Colonel, my governess had a word for you.'

'Yes,' I said. 'But I've a wife and family.'

'Right! Seen it a dozen times. Just love and kisses, and a man's a bloody hero. Give him a couple of children and he's got to know what he's fighting for. Now, you're in this, but if I'm not wrong – and when I'm talking to a born soldier I'm never wrong – I don't believe you know what you're in or why.'

I didn't reply. The general's intuition or judgment of character was far too dangerous.

'Now, how am I going to put it?' he went on. 'Ever read state trials? Russia and elsewhere?'

'I used to.'

'Don't wonder you stopped! Think the evidence is all faked, ha? Well, it isn't. Men who confess they are guilty *are* guilty. What of? There we have it! Guilty of muddle. And it doesn't take any drugs or tortures to make them confess it. Of course they are muddled. Why? Because the bosses are muddled. There's no firm creed. That's the thing to remember. A creed is what the leader says it is, and no more.

'That makes it easy to muscle in on the racket. Just like Hitler and Mussolini. You have to start as a socialist – that's all – and then you have to muddle. Tell the working man that you're going to avoid all the errors of communism and democracy, and that you're just going to exercise a little benevolent dictatorship until things are running properly.

'And that, colonel, my lad, is what is going on. Party here, party there, all supporting each other all over Europe. Couriers, money, beautiful agreements on paper. It's nothing but a new fascism.'

'You're employed by your government?' I asked.

'Colonel, I would be shot on sight if I set foot in Poland.'

'Then revolution ought to suit you.'

'Well, it doesn't. Revolution would be the end of Poland. We Poles are all patriots, even the communists. We play for time. We wait for destiny. We want stability. A group of Hitlers, all jumping up simultaneously, all promising peace and plenty, where would that get you or me, ha?

I tell you, there's one of 'em ready in every country from Georgia to Ireland.'

'Who's ours?' I asked sceptically. 'Pink?'

'Pink? These men are near the top! All of them different kinds of socialist. I don't know yet who yours is. Might be ...' and he mentioned three ministers, each of whom, certainly, was so mystically sure of his own rightness and benevolence that he would have qualified as a budding Hitler.

'Ever heard of Robert Heyne-Hassingham?' I asked.

He had; but the name meant little to him. He only knew, through his investigations into the neo-fascist cells abroad, that there was a corresponding underground in England, and that it carried on under cover of some respectable movement.

'Or of a Colonel Hiart?'

'Hiart? Head of your intelligence service in ... during the war. What's he doing now? Brilliant fellow but crazy with nerves. Hated firearms because they went bang. Always seeing assassins under his bed, ha?'

'The sort of chap who might imagine General Sandorski when the general was on the other side of the Channel?'

'Colonel, I order you – I beg you, tell me what you know.'

'I know something damned odd is going on over my shoot,' I replied. 'And that's all. Where are you staying?'

'The mental hospital,' he announced with a sly pride. 'My doctor is there.'

All my original doubts came back.

'Of course,' I agreed. 'They are right up to date.'

He leapt to his feet in a passion, and popped down again as flat on his face as if he had just been missed by a sniper.

'Chap up there,' he said.

I raised a cautious head and peered through the furze. There was indeed a chap up there, going for a leisurely country walk. I recognized him at once as the man who had watched Blossom's gate and bridge.

'When I say my doctor,' Sandorski hissed, 'I mean my doctor before the war. If I were mad, you bloody fool, would they have made me a general?'

'I don't know,' I said. 'I've never studied the Polish campaign.'

That went right over his head. He was much too angry. When the walker had passed us and was safely out of earshot, he told me that his pre-war doctor had joined the staff of the Dorset Mental Hospital with a bunch of other highly qualified refugees from Poland and Lithuania; till he learned English, he was acting only as a superior orderly, but he had a pleasant cottage in the grounds, and there was no reason in the world why he shouldn't have a friend to stay with him.

Sandorski's improvisation was brilliant, and he had every right to be proud of it. The Mental Hospital was a self-contained world, and neither police nor Heyne-Hassingham would ever bother about its guests. One just didn't think of it as having any. Moreover, if some interested person noticed anything eccentric in Sandorski's behaviour and chose to watch him – as easily I might myself – his disappearance into those well-kept grounds would effectively stop further inquiries.

'Can I see you there?' I asked.

'Why not? Any time you like.'

'Be there between nine and ten tomorrow.'

And I told him that he mustn't go near my house which might be watched. I also warned him that he might be seen by someone who knew him.

'Colonel, my lad,' he replied superbly, 'you are an infantryman. When the cavalry charges, it is always likely to be seen.'

Well, that was fine when he was all alone and deliberately provoking any sort of incident that would reveal the enemy. I suggested, however, that since his dash and tactics had been so successful, the cavalry, for the moment, had better go into reserve.

'And now do something for me,' I asked. 'Telephone this number and tell my wife that Mr Taine won't be back till after dark, and tell her that they tried oil on the ants who complained it was the wrong grade for summer.'

He was very suspicious. After all, I had explained nothing.

'Just a father's ruse to prove his identity,' I assured him.

I showed him a route back to the loony-bin, where he would be safe from observation till he was well away from Blossom's farm.

I myself went off in the opposite direction, for I was

interested by that country walker. I saw him finish his stroll along the edge of the escarpment, and vanish into a little copse at the point where the slope curved round to the east. I hurried after, keeping well under the brow of the hill where he couldn't see me, and reached a clump of rough stuff below and outside the copse.

He was, as I expected, just within the trees – an excellent position from which he could watch the road at the bottom of the valley and the green track along the top. Once or twice he raised his field-glasses to examine traffic on the road. Apart from that slight movement he was so absorbed by duty that an incautious rabbit put its head out of a bramble bush within five yards of him.

That was a wonderful chance to study his reactions. I shot the rabbit dead, and had the satisfaction of seeing him jump and drop his glasses. He didn't make any instinctive leap for cover, however, so it was reasonably clear he had heard nothing of any acts of violence in the neighbourhood.

'By Jove!' I exclaimed. 'I'm sorry! I didn't see you.'

I picked up the rabbit, and smiled at him with what I hoped was an expression of innocence and concern.

'This is intolerable,' he complained. 'Intolerable! Careless brutality! Have you no thought at all of the suffering you cause to harmless creatures?'

His voice was like the whine of a bagpipe, and his little feet danced to it with indignation.

'We all must eat,' I said.

'Have you not enough to eat with what the government allows you? A carefully balanced diet approved by all the statisticians? Killing for food should be left to those who can distribute economically, and understand it.'

'At least I understand it,' I replied with a grin, swinging the rabbit at him. 'He didn't suffer at all.'

'Improper!' he squealed.

'Is your objection on religious grounds?'

'Certainly not. I have no religion. My objection is that these sports of the rich, these remnants of feudalism, are anti-social.'

'But I'm not rich.'

'Then if you are not, you should set an example.'

He was a lovely little man. I didn't want to lose him till he had told me everything he knew; so I apologized and asked to be shown the light. He recommended several pamphlets which, I gathered, pleaded for the trap as more humane than the gun. I promised to read them. Then I asked him if he were on holiday.

'As much as I allow myself,' he replied. 'I am studying the collection of essential statistics for a backward rural area.'

'Splendid! Who for?'

'The Workers' Improvement Society.'

'A labour organization?'

'Certainly not! It is one of the extra-parliamentary activities of the People's Union.'

You had only to see him, to hear his limited little mind

at talk, to know that he couldn't be anything else but sincere. He was just the sort of chap who could be employed for any dirty trick with absolute confidence that he wouldn't see it so long as he felt useful and important. I am sure I should have accepted him at face value if I hadn't known better, and especially if I hadn't known – for about an hour – that the People's Union under Heyne-Hassingham was subtle and dangerous at home and abroad as the young Nazi or Communist parties.

'What are you checking up here?' I asked.

'Parallel movement, and the proportion of pedestrians and transport using a non-metalled track in preference to a secondary road, and their reasons. I shall put down your own reason as the destruction of wildlife.'

'Call it rodent control,' I answered. 'What do you do with your statistics when you've got them?'

'A colleague of mine correlates them.'

'And anyone out for a country walk – how does he fit in?'

'I ask him firmly what he is doing,' he replied, 'and explain my motives with official courtesy. If in fact he is going for a country walk, I make a note of his income bracket and description, and enter his name in the column Non-Economic Activities.'

'How long have you been at it?'

'Since October 19th.'

'Description of every person seen, ha?'

I had caught that confounded *ha?* from Sandorski.

'I am assured it is essential to avoid duplication.'

'Sounds as if you were being trained for the police,' I said.

He blushed, positively blushed. Blowed if I hadn't penetrated the secret hopes that had been held out to him!

'The police are politically untrained and unreliable,' he spluttered.

It was enough. I couldn't have kept a straight face any longer – though it was really a matter for tears that such a man could ask his silly questions and be treated with deference in our once merry England. I said good-bye, renewed my apologies, and kept him under observation from a distance. I didn't have to wait long. He marched down to the village, as importantly as the steep slope allowed.

Since listening to Sandorski I had made a pretty confident guess at what the value of my shoot was to the interested parties. Sandorski had talked quite casually of agents being flown in and out of England. The newspapers, too, often carried stories of smuggling by air, and of the difficulty of police and Customs control. The down was no landing field, but there was a level strip a good third of a mile long, with a rough but well-drained surface. It was quite good enough for any aircraft with a low landing speed. I also remembered Heyne-Hassingham's conversation with Blossom. Hadn't he been very anxious to know that there were no sheep or cattle on the down?

It was dusk, the best time to see and not be seen. I didn't

dare to approach the angle of the hedge where the dead man had been busy with his spirit level and spiked supports. Lord knew what ingenious devices there might be to record, the passage of anyone pottering about! I decided, however, that I might risk a look at the northern end of the supposed airstrip. The uninterrupted level passed diagonally across the shoot, and ended in that kaffir kraal of domed bramble bushes from which Pink and his late thug had been coming when they surprised me.

I knew more or less where to search – where the longest possible level line from the fatal angle of the hedge intersected the southern edge of the brambles. That wasn't so vague as it sounds, for the clumps, when you got among them, were widely separated, and there weren't more than half a dozen on the likely line.

I found what I wanted, a bush with the interior hollowed out. The entrance was well hidden, and to be detected only by the trampled grass. A casual eye would have put the disturbance down to cows. There were plenty of them munching the short turf here on the safe side of the hedge, where they couldn't get in the way of a whirling propeller.

Inside the bush was enough empty space for a man to kneel without getting thorns in his head or twigs down his collar. The light, which outside was fast fading, was a deep elephant grey, revealing neither outline nor perspective. I hadn't a torch with me, so I lit match after match, placing the burnt ends carefully in my pocket. The hole had been cleaned up – so far as it was possible to clean a floor of indefinite vegetable debris – but I got my evidence: half an inch of insulated copper wire, a bit of thin broken glass that suggested a bulb or radio valve, four holes in the ground, and some filings and chips of bright metal that would have been indistinguishable in daylight, and twinkled like stars in the light of a match.

Then, pushing accidentally against the side of the hollow, I found still clearer and wholly unsuspected evidence. There was a little alcove or bay, stuffed up with dead bramble stalks. I parted them carefully and saw, driven into the ground and levelled, four supports, identical with those I had buried by the side of their owner in the rabbit warren, all ready for what they were to hold.

Now I had a picture and the beginning of a pattern, and immediately the dull weight upon my conscience vanished. Whether morally it should have done so, I doubt; for I was neither more nor less guilty than before of causing the death of a man. But, from this moment on, crime assumed the amoral, inconsequent quality of a death that one has caused in war.

When I got home – after some cautious reconnaissance to ensure that nobody was interested in the time I returned – I was horrified to notice how drawn and weary my Cecily looked. She must have had that worry upon her face for a couple of weeks, and I hadn't noticed it. It would be truer to say that I hadn't wished to notice it. I had a wild romp with Jerry and George, and was told off by her in the normal way for exciting them before they went to bed. There was a note of relief in her half-angry protest. The house seemed to have returned to its accustomed casual happiness.

'Your friend has a nice voice,' she said to me when we were alone, 'but he shouldn't pretend to be English.'

'Good lord, he could pass anywhere!'

'Not with women. He's too gallant.'

'On the telephone?'

'He told me what I looked like from the way I spoke.'

'And do you?'

'I hope so,' she laughed.

Then she started to talk of our friends, flitting inconsequently from one to another. It was that sort of monologue to which a husband can go on answering *hm* and *ah* so long as he takes care to look intelligent and interested. What did I think of this one and that? And their wives? And their daughters? I tried not to show that most of them bored me, for that might have reflected upon Cecily's ability to make them interesting – and small blame to her, for even their Maker had failed! It was only after half an hour of this that I spotted she was trying to find out – from my enthusiasm or studied carelessness - whether I wasn't running some clandestine affair under cover of the pretended building racket.

I kept this brilliant discovery to myself, for I didn't want to hurt her pride. If a woman has pride and joy, you cannot help loving her. I suppose they all know that, and rather wish they didn't.

In the morning – much to her annoyance on a Sunday – I had business between nine and ten. I called on Sandorski and found him in a turtle-neck sweater glowing with foxy health after, no doubt, some crazily strenuous daily dozen and a hearty lunatic's breakfast. His host, the doctor, having been on night duty, was asleep.

'My shoot,' I told him, 'is a landing ground. They mean to put movable radio beacons at both ends of the strip. When you shot that friend of yours he was arranging an emplacement for the southern beacon. The strip has not yet been used, but it's going to be. It's high ground clear of obstructions, remote, level, and the landowner is in this up to his neck.'

'It won't be used,' he answered, 'because they know somebody found them out.'

'Nobody found them out. They have been wondering whether I mightn't be guilty. If it wasn't me, it could be a poacher.'

I decided to trust him. It was pointless to go on mystifying a wholehearted ally who had hidden little or nothing from me. I told him how the accident really happened. He guffawed at my words of regret.

'Lord!' he yelled, 'I once did the same thing to my uncle! Lord! We both had our breakfast off the mantelpiece for weeks!'

Then he bounced about like a little boy with an urgent need, shouting:

'Air pistol! Air pistol! Air pistol!'

'Mean anything to you?'

'Riemann! That's the man you shot. Colonel, my lad, if Riemann has had it, you've done me a favour. Now, whom was he with?'

'Your Colonel Hiart,' I replied, 'if it's the same colonel you knew. Tall, thin, sunburnt, dark. Very sensitive and intelligent face. Can stand still indefinitely, which most people can't. And likely to know that Peter Sandorski was after his companion.'

'That's him! No soldier – never was! But knows everything! Guesses what I'm working on. Guesses I might catch up with Riemann any day. General of Cavalry – that would frighten him, ha? Second sight, but a bloody pansy . . .' and he went into details.

'But you grant him a flair?'

'Cleverest man in Europe, when he isn't too scared to think.'

'Right! Now, suppose he went over the ground in daylight, there must have been plenty of evidence for a trained eye. I don't believe I ever picked up the empty cartridge. And when he'd pulled himself together, he might remember the difference of sound between a gun and a rifle. Damn it, he's a soldier, and he must have heard plenty of both, even if he doesn't like 'em! And wouldn't he check up where you were at the time? It's a fair old puzzle, but he ought to know the death or disappearance of Riemann had nothing to do with the airstrip.'

'Hiart, ha?' he answered, as if the man's reactions were not to be judged by ordinary standards. 'You or a poacher at eighty yards? It might occur to him. But he wouldn't rule out straight revenge on Riemann. And I don't think they'll use the airstrip.'

'Then why have they put back the supports for the beacon?'

'How do you know they ever took 'em away?'

'Because they'd have taken a horrid risk if they didn't, and because I've seen the four holes where the spikes were before. That's what Pink and your S. S. man were doing just before they nearly caught me – pulling up the supports and hiding them somewhere.'

He snorted agreement.

'Who's employing Hiart?' he asked.

I gave him a picture of Heyne-Hassingham and a lecture on the People's Union, bringing in the earnest statistician as an example. It all fitted – an organization at bottom hysterical, but in practice efficient, impudent and with an appeal to the ruthless idealist.

'The rest, during the week, is up to you, General,' I said, 'because I have to earn my living. What we want to know is when those beacons go into position. And I'll tell you what time to watch. Not in daylight, because there are too many people about. Not at night because they won't want to show a lot of artificial light. But at dusk, after the farm labourers have gone home. And I think they'll also want to be sure that I am in my office and not taking an afternoon off.'

'And what then?'

'We go to the police, I suppose.'

'Any evidence?'

'The beacons.'

'Colonel, my lad,' he smiled, 'just work it out! What will the police do? Send up a couple of constables to check your story. Somebody will see 'em or hear 'em, and that's the end of the airstrip.

'What's the next move, ha? Anonymous information to the police that Colonel Taine may be using his shoot as a little private Garden of Remembrance. With all the details. You try and deny 'em. Especially if they say you bumped him off on the 19th, when the motorcycle was found, not the 18th. Where's your alibi? What's your story? People's Union? You must be a political maniac. Heyne-Hassingham and Hiart? Above suspicion! Where did you put that body, by the way?'

'Where it will take a lot of finding,' I answered sulkily.

'Think so? I've had some experience. So has Scotland Yard. I'll tell you the alternatives. Under the manure heap in the barn. In the middle of a bush – but unless you were in a tearing hurry, we'll rule that out. Any heap of stones. Or the pit where the dead sheep are. Ha? Ha, pokerface? Now, you leave it all to me.'

Sandorski pointed out that for a job of this kind – and

he said he had organized enough of them to know – an aircraft had to have a fairly respectable base and a reason for leaving it. Therefore it would take off in daylight. Therefore it would arrive before midnight. And if it were going to land within five hundred yards of a road, the organizers must be sure of a dark night with no moon. That gave Wednesday, Thursday or Friday as the most likely dates. He didn't think they would risk leaving the beacons in position; they would bring them out to the field on the night the plane was expected. I was just, he repeated, to leave it to him.

I did so, with some misgivings on the Polish Cavalry's conception of intelligence work. Colonel Hiart, with his extreme caution, seemed a more desirable model. We agreed that Sandorski would telephone me at my home if the beacons were put up, and that I would join him within an hour at the haystacks above Blossom's farmhouse – a rendezvous which both of us felt certain we could reach in darkness without being observed. Just in case they had a man to spare for watching my door, I said I would go out at the back and walk across the hills to the shoot.

On the Wednesday, soon after I returned to the office from lunch, I had a telephone call from someone who sounded like a harassed and indecisive farmer and asked me if I would be in at five as he wished to consult me about new types of porous flooring for poultry runs. He seemed to be in a great hurry and rang off without giving his name. When nobody turned up at five, it occurred to me that the caller intended to find out whether I should be safely in my office at dusk. It was a very useful warning that something might happen. I prepared the way for plenty of free time by telling my clerk that I felt rotten and thought I might be starting a go of 'flu.

I went home in a curious mood of high hopes and misgivings. It's no good to deny it. A family man, however contented, does like a bit of excitement if he's ever been used to any.

About seven my telephone rang and I jumped to it. Cecily, who always answers the telephone (since nine-tenths of the calls are for her), gave me a startled smile. She had convinced herself, I think, that the building materials racket was over.

'All set to go,' said Sandorski's voice. 'How are the ants? Here's a horn for their car!'

And he blew a colossal raspberry that must have nearly wrecked the diaphragm of my telephone.

'Have you a pistol?' he asked.

I replied that I hadn't. As a matter of fact, I had. I was reluctant to part with an old wartime friend, though to retain it was downright illegal. But I did not want to put myself into temptation. I had enough trouble as it was.

I warned Cecily that if anyone called or telephoned she was to say I had gone to bed with a touch of 'flu and was asleep.

'Darling, don't forget there are three of us who depend on you,' she said.

I told her I never thought of anything else.

I slipped out of the back door, crossed the meadows and waded the stream. As the crow flies the distance to Blossom's farm wasn't more than three miles, but the crow didn't make Dorset footpaths, and I had to step out smartly to reach the haystacks in an hour.

It was a blustery evening with a few fierce showers and comparative calm between. The weather report was of strong winds over the North Sea, rising at times to gale force. With us it was a good enough night for a clandestine landing, but I didn't think it would appear so at the point of departure.

After crossing a steep little green range, I sploshed down a muddy cart-track and hit the lower road south of Blossom's house. I hoped that statistician was there in the rain, taking a census of labourers returning from the village pub. Then I turned off into a dry valley which led up to the back of the shoot. My feet on the turf made no sound. It was very dark, and a solid object could only be distinguished thirty yards away. I knew that I couldn't be observed or followed.

I arrived at the stacks silently and on the hour. I couldn't see Sandorski, and he gave me the worst fright of the evening when he spoke from the level of my feet. He was lying on an old tarpaulin, which I had already touched to be sure that tarpaulin it was, and absolutely invisible.

He told me that the beacons had been set up at dusk, just as I had prophesied; they were, he thought, of transpontor type, and each had been easily carried by two men. All this he had seen from the top of a beech in the boundary hedge, where he had been on watch every afternoon and evening. After it was darkish, he had heard the party going back to the upper road. Thereupon he trotted down to the village to telephone me.

'Any plan?' I asked.

'Not yet. What are we up against? Don't know!'

We took position not far from the southern beacon. About nine we heard their footsteps. They must have moved very quietly as far as the boundary hedge. Then they had to cross a strip of ploughland strewn with large flints. I had never discovered a way of walking silently over those flints, and nor did they.

So far as we could tell, they crossed the plough and settled down somewhere on the edge of the grass. Since I knew every foot of the surface and Sandorski did not, I left him in our hiding-place and explored, stopping frequently to listen. I spotted them first by the flare of a match. They felt confident enough to smoke. I crawled over the turf till I was within twenty yards of them. They were still a party of four. In the glow of the cigarette ends I felt pretty certain that I recognized Hiart.

Their voices were low, and I could only distinguish a few sentences in the hush between the passing gusts of wind. I should have said the hush was complete, but when one tried to listen there were smaller breezes playing through the dead thistle stalks, or the flap of their mackintoshes; or, just as a whisper was giving the clue to previous half-guessed words, the tiny crepitation of insect or field mouse close to my ear. I gathered, at any rate, that the plane was starting from Austria, that it would refuel in France on the return journey, and that they too, thought it wouldn't come. They were prepared to wait for it again on the following night.

I returned to the general with my news. We sat where we were, and about an hour before midnight someone came to the beacon and presumably switched off the battery. He didn't go through the gap in the boundary hedge and off to the road, but back to rejoin the rest of his party on the down. Sandorski leapt at the opportunity to get away before them, see what was the number of their car, and whether there was anyone waiting in it.

It was too bold, even on so dark a night, for after we passed the gap they weren't more than a hundred yards behind us. We silently increased our lead and then, finding no car at all at the junction of the track and the upper road, dropped into the ditch and let them pass us. We trailed them at a reasonable distance – at least it seemed reasonable to Sandorski – and discovered that they had left their car half a mile down the road, just up a little metalled track which ran through a patch of woodland. When they drove away, there were still only four men in the car, so we knew that it had been left unguarded. The People's Union, for all its thousands of innocent enthusiasts, seemed to be a bit short of manpower for a job of this delicacy.

I slept deeply and late, foreseeing that the next night I might have little chance, and at my office pretended to be bravely carrying on in spite of that incipient 'flu. My clerk was sympathetic. It may seem unnecessarily grand for a plain salesman to boast a clerk – but we had a few big contracts, and I needed someone to sit within reach of the telephone when I was out. The job suited him. He was over sixty, reliable and fatherly. He said that my eyes were altogether too clear and bright, and that I looked like an aunt of his just before she died. It might, I thought, well be so. I've seen plenty of men whose eyes were clear and bright just before they died. Only they didn't know they were going to.

His confounded aunt put ideas into my head. I wrote down for Cecily a short account of what had happened, sealed it up, and took the envelope round to the bank. I didn't feel the office safe was secure enough.

In the evening I played with the boys, and ate an early supper. I told Cecily that I had to go out, and that I hoped this would be the last night of the investigation. She didn't know quite what to make of my mood, for I was in good spirits. It seemed to me more and more unlikely that I should ever be in the dock for manslaughter. Anything else that was coming to me I could handle.

Soon after half-past seven I was with Sandorski, tucked into the hedge above the southern beacon. An hour later the party arrived, and stood quite close to us while they checked and switched on the beacon. Pink and Hiart we recognized beyond doubt. The other two were unknown to either of us. They were not as careful as they had been the night before. Growing familiarity with the job, perhaps. And really there was no reason why they should be careful. It was a million to one against anybody being out of doors on the open ground of Blossom's and the adjoining farm.

The night was clear, with a niggling north-west wind which was damp and cold out of all proportion to its strength. The four men didn't lie out again on the edge of their airstrip; they retired to the comfortable shelter of the boundary hedge.

It was their distance from the beacons and the top of the down that gave Sandorski his crazy inspiration. He suddenly slapped me on the back.

'Why not?' he asked me in a yell of a whisper. 'Why not?'

His tone was all full of irresponsible cavalry tactics. I wouldn't have been surprised if he suggested chasing Hiart over the downs with a lance. I replied that I'd tell him why not at once, if I knew what he was proposing.

'Why not shift the beacons?'

'Wreck the plane?'

'Hell, no! Welcome it! Reception committee, ha? We ought to have three minutes. Might have much more.'

I protested at the outrageous gamble.

'Gamble? What gamble? They can't know the plane is

coming down in the wrong place till it's down there.'

'But why? What's the objective?'

'Muck 'em up! What else? Sit on our backsides in a bramble bush? Just see him land and take off again? Pah! That's what Hiart would do. We want to know what or whom they are flying over. Well, go and grab the lot. Can't do any harm.'

'Oh, can't it!' I said.

'What? Still thinking of Riemann's home from home? Good God, man, are you going to put your miserable private affairs before service to your country?'

I never in my life heard such a lousy argument. I was still by no means convinced that I was serving my country, and even less that his wild scheme would benefit anyone but the four men waiting in the boundary hedge. Yet he left me with no possible reply. I didn't wonder the Poles made him a general. He could only be that or a trooper. All other ranks are supposed to think with their brains.

'Now where shall we make the poor beggar land?' he asked cheerfully, as if it were all settled.

'There's only one possible place. Where the down continues the other side of the northern hedge. But there are cows there.'

'Well, if he hits one, he hits one. What do you know about radio beacons?'

'Nothing.'

'Stands to reason that if they work in one place, they work in another. Ha? Doesn't it? And they can be dropped by parachute and work – I know that. So if we carry 'em carefully and level 'em up, we ought to be all right.'

'Suppose they come and look at them again?'

'Well, they didn't last night, so why should they tonight?'

'Have we time?' I protested as a last effort.

'Not if you stand there,' he hissed, 'arguing in bloody whispers all night.'

We lifted the southern beacon and its supports and made a detour round the landing strip, following the grass track along the edge of the down below which I had sat with Sandorski on the day of our meeting. The lights twinkled in the village below, and the headlights of cars flicked their white sheets over trees and stream. All the time I listened for the plane. Once we both cursed, but it was an air-liner on its way to the north.

We set up the beacon in the northern hedge. The supports were admirably fitted for their purpose. Their sharp points bit firmly into the turf of the bank; with two long legs, one short and one slightly shorter, we had the thing straight enough for any practical use.

In that dark kaffir kraal of bramble bushes it wasn't so easy to find the other beacon, and the time was now half-past nine. We made a lot of impatient noise, but the party sitting in the boundary hedge was too far away to hear us. At last we got it and fixed it up on the very brink of the valley. Here the steep escarpment swept round to the east, abruptly ending Blossom's down. We could only give that unknown and unfortunate pilot something under four hundred yards, instead of the five to six hundred that the proper reception committee had allowed. After we got the beacon in position I paced out the distance and shifted a couple of sleepy cows. There were no other obstacles so long as the pilot stayed bang on his line and could stop before he plunged into the valley.

We then had time to sit down and work out the odds. If the plane landed according to the signals from the beacons, and if it didn't go over the edge – two very big ifs – we had rather more than the three minutes which Peter Sandorski had demanded. The four men in the boundary hedge would come up to the level of their airstrip when they expected or heard the plane, but even there they would be a quarter of a mile from us, plus the distance that the plane travelled. When the pilot overshot their strip, they would think he meant to turn and come back, so that they wouldn't begin to run up until he actually landed. Sandorski's plan began to look less like a nightmare.

A little after ten the plane circled once, and came in over the hedge like a great silent owl. The pilot revved up as he touched, and taxied forward till his wing was nearly over the beacon. He saw or sensed the appalling drop in front of him, lurched round, switched on his light and spent an intolerable time manoeuvring into a position where there wasn't a cow or a thorn bush or sudden death in front of him.

As soon as his wheels came to rest he put out his light. I suppose he had been instructed not to use it, and to trust to beacon signals. We hammered excitedly on the door. Sandorski left it to me to do the talking in case his voice should be recognized. I sounded, he said, just like any other blasted Englishman. The rest of him was safely unrecognizable. In the dark he was a shapeless mass of sweaters and wind-breakers, and his small head was extinguished between cap and muffler.

The door was opened from within, and a man peered doubtfully out into the night.

'Quick!' I shouted. 'We haven't a moment. Police on the way! Jump, man!'

He dropped to the ground, carrying a small suitcase with him.

'Anything else?'

'It is all,' the stranger answered.

The pilot stuck his head out.

'Here!' he protested. 'Call this a landing strip? Not again! I'm not a—'

'Get out of here, you fool!' I yelled hysterically. 'You'll be arrested in a minute. Get out!'

'What's ahead?'

'Three hundred yards and then a hedge. Jump it if you can't fly it.'

'Cripes!' he said. 'I'll bring a horse next time.'

We had created a fine atmosphere of alarm and despondency. The plane roared and began to move. The pilot flooded the turf with light again and revealed the real reception committee running towards us less than a hundred yards away. With the engine ticking over, it had been impossible for us to hear their movements.

He took no risk of being stopped. I wonder he didn't kill the lot of them. But he cleared the hedge. While we ran I heard the steady drone of the plane in its safe and lonely world, and envied him.

We took the nearest way, straight down the slope. That for the moment increased our lead, and I got rid of the passenger's suitcase into a thick holly which I knew I could find again even in the dark. Relieved of that, he ran like a man with a guilty conscience.

We swerved back, following the contour line below the copse where my innocent statistician had sat and counted traffic and began to pound up the slope at an angle. This was stumbling, not running; and our pursuers drew up into close touch. They couldn't see us – or only as occasional bulks against the sky – but they couldn't fail to hear us.

They had had time to think and began to call:

'Lex! Lex!'

'That vos the voice of Peenk,' said the passenger in a firm Central European accent, and half stopping.

I shoved him on.

'Run, Lex! Pink's the police informer. I'm getting you to Heyne-Hassingham.'

Thank the Lord he was high up in the party! That name seemed to be immediate proof of my bona fides. He crashed along the side of that hill like a startled heifer, through bush and over rabbit-hole. We increased our lead a bit, and I took a chance on being where I thought I was. I pulled them round behind a thorn brake, through a gap in the furze and down on to the ground. As we dropped flat on the turf, Lex gave a muffled cry of pain.

'Damn these thorns!' hissed Sandorski.

He dug me in the ribs and held out, behind our friend's back, a little syringe with which he had just jabbed him in the thigh.

The hunt passed us, then checked and turned back. They knew, as soon as they stopped to listen, that we must have gone to ground on the hillside. In the stillness of the night you could hear a man charging across country half a mile away. If only we could have reached the springy turf of the green track above us, we could have run – or jumped or danced, for that matter – without a sound.

They closed in and flashed torches quickly on and off. They were wise not to spoil their night sight, and it may be, too, that they feared we were armed and desperate. All they could see was a formless black mass of thorn and furze, forbidding search. The twisting track into the heart of it, worn down by the persistent feet of little animals and an occasional sheep, was clear enough from where we lay, but indistinguishable from outside. Two of them were above us and two below us. They made a half-hearted attempt to beat the patch, but the furze was stiff and centuries old; we might have been surrounded by a lion-proof thorn fence.

It was as well that Sandorski's syringe had done its work, for they started to ask Lex what the devil he thought he was doing. They couldn't say very much, for they didn't know who was with him or why the plane had come down in the wrong place, or why it had immediately and frantically taken off again. Indeed, they couldn't be certain that Lex had ever got out of the plane at all – and from their point of view we might be three unknown enemies, or Lex and two. Sandorski's cavalry tactics had landed us in the most god-awful defenceless position, but at least they had bewitched the opposing force into a nightmare world where nothing made sense.

Hiart's querulous voice, above us, said:

'For heaven's sake, don't go throwing names about!'

Pink, from below us and in a furious temper, told him to beggar off home to his bleeding nanny.

All the same, it wasn't funny. True, they couldn't see us till they stepped on us, but they had only to wait till daylight or till we grew impatient.

We heard somebody moving round our patch of cover and giving orders in whispers. I think it was Hiart, for their next move showed a certain subtlety. They shifted noisily about until we hadn't the faintest notion where any single one of them was, and then preserved the most absolute, disciplined silence.

We were out of the wind in that slope, and there wasn't a sound. A rare car rushed along the road in the valley beneath. A sheep coughed on the lower ground by the stream. This went on for half an hour. At least I found it to be only half an hour when I looked at my watch. I thought it must be nearly dawn. Strain on the nerves has no time.

Then Lex began to thrash about in his dreamland, and somebody above us closed in towards the sound. I hung on to Lex's legs and Sandorski lay across his chest and arms. Pink must have been near enough to hear Lex's heavy breathing. He shot in our general direction and scored a bull. He hit the rectangle between Sandorski's legs, Lex's body and my arms. It wasn't his fault that there was nothing but turf in it.

The shot was the breaking point for somebody else who had been frozen and terrified like ourselves. A roe deer, away to our left in a patch of thick stuff where one of us easily might have been but was not, broke cover and crashed away. Sandorski, instantaneously appreciating what the enemy would infer, broke cover too and went after it, drawing off two of the watchers; they might, if he had given them a moment to think, have spotted the first disturbance as that of an animal, but they couldn't distinguish the noises – since one was followed so immediately by another – and could only assume that two of us had gone.

Right! Make it a third, I thought! And down the hill I went – after, of course, the interval of some seconds which I needed to catch up with Sandorski's brilliance. I drew off the other two sentries, one of whom was Pink. His naval language was unmistakable. I led them up again to the turf, and there, where I could run silently, easily lost them.

I listened. I could hear Pink and his companion blundering through a bit of heavy ploughland that lay between me and the airstrip. I guessed that he had given up the pursuit as hopeless – which it was – and was returning to the party's rendezvous under the boundary hedge.

There was no knowing what Sandorski would do, for we had not arranged any rendezvous at all. Whether he heard my escape or not, however, it wasn't likely he would lose touch for long with the unconscious Lex. Meanwhile the position was chaotic. Scattered over half a square mile of down and plough and thicket were Sandorski and myself and the disorganized reception committee, none of us knowing where the others were, and all anxious to find out. Additional complications were Lex snoring in the bushes and his bag in the holly tree.

Lex gave a heave and a rumble. In the night silence which had now become more absolute and hostile than ever, that noise seemed as outrageous a signal as any flashing light. I decided to shift him at once, while I could be sure that my own section of empty space was really empty. I carried him down the hill and left him in the open, where his odd noises would sound like those of the sheep, memorizing his position as well as I could without any very definite landmarks to go by.

I settled down on the edge of the turf track above our temporary hiding place. After a bit, Hiart, tall enough to recognize, came flitting cautiously over the grass with one of his men. They stopped and listened at the right spot, gave it up and vanished northwards along the track.

Where were they going? Well, if Hiart had the intelligence Sandorski attributed to him – and I was immensely impressed by his finding, in a world that all looked alike, the exact patch where we had been – then he would guess that the only explanation of the aircraft coming down in the wrong place and being expected there by unknown persons must be that the beacons had been moved. Having checked that, he would try to find them – for they were evidence that must at all costs be removed – and carry them off to his car. It wouldn't take him long to discover the one in the open on the edge of the slope, and then the tracks of the landing wheels would lead him somewhere near the other in the hedge.

I hoped that Sandorski might be close behind Hiart, but he was not. I waited and waited, feeling all the time that we might be within a few yards of each other, and each afraid to break the silence. I needn't have worried. When Sandorski did come, it was boldly clown the track, and singing in a low, but not nearly low enough, voice some preposterous chorus:

'One day in October
I wasn't so sober.'

'For the Lord's sake!' I protested.

'English folk-song,' he answered. 'Learned it from my

72

governess. They're miles away and busy. Have a cigarette!'

'Where are they?'

'Looking for the beacons, all four of them.'

'That won't take them long.'

'Won't it, ha? One is half-way down the hill, and the other on its side under a pile of cabbage.'

'Kale.'

'Well, whatever damned kraut you feed the cows in this country. Next thing, Colonel, my lad, is to restore your temper.'

'What's the matter with it?'

'Our friend under the daisies. Dig him up, and you're a free man.'

Even in the midst of this excitement I wasn't very ready to give away the place. So long as I kept my precious secret to myself it was secure.

'You bloody fool!' he said. 'Now's your chance to do what you ought to have done the first time. Burn their car and burn him in it. They'll think the corpse is Lex. That'll keep Hiart quiet! That'll make him stay at home. Suspicion? Nonsense! Why you? Life's wide open to inspection. Decent bourgeois selling tombstones. No connection whatever with Poles and such. Continent isolated, ha?'

It did look, I must admit, as if I were on to a good thing. I led Sandorski to the rabbit warren. It was a little close to the hedge where the beacon lay under its pile of kale, but Hiart's party were at the far end of the down still searching for the other.

At the bottom of the pit we could safely use a torch. We dug him out with our hands, and I left him to Sandorski for I didn't want to look. I smoothed back the earth and arranged the fallen thorn in its old position.

Sandorski flashed his light on what had been the face. It didn't tell him anything but the common fate of man. He looked further, and found a tattoo mark on the right arm and a locket or identity disc on a light chain round the neck. He took it and put it in his pocket.

'So that is the end of Riemann,' he said.

It was he who had the courage to deal with the corpse, he who was glad to see the man dead. Yet there was a sob in his voice.

'What had he done?' I asked.

'Despaired. Wanted a short cut and thought we were too patient. Went over to these people and broke open my organization, for I had trusted him. Not for money and not for country, but just because he thought they were the saviours of the future. Taine, I find myself against every kind of idealism.'

It was a terrible confession to cry out, but, in this world of passionately sincere political creeds, it was true. He was in opposition to them all. Yet he had an ideal, and it was Christendom, the holy and forgotten unity of Europe. Only in such a Europe, where politics were seen to be a mere expedient compared to the beauty of the common heritage, could his people live.

He took out a knife and removed all traces of lead pellets

74

from the body. I could see none, but we had to expect the microscopes of a police laboratory. Then he pulled the leg of the beacon from Riemann's heart and buried it again.

'Hang on to his heels,' he said.

We trotted along the boundary hedge to the gap, and when we reached the upper road followed it down to the patch of woodland where they had left their car the previous night. We took to the ditch once when the headlights of a lorry, climbing the hill, swept and wavered through the sky. Otherwise we didn't see a sign of man.

The car was again unguarded. Hiart must have been very nervous about it, but he had no reason to suppose we knew where it was. And in any case he couldn't spare a man.

We wrenched off the main petrol lead, bent it and soaked Riemann and the floor mats. Then we put him in the driving seat, and Sandorski threw a lighted cigarette into the pool of petrol beneath the car. The result was spectacular. We were only just far enough away.

We cleared out, back along the hard road where our footprints wouldn't show, then over a wire fence on to firm grass, and so across country to Blossom's land, which we hit near his hill-top barn. The glare lit up our eastern horizon. I don't know what the party at the northern end of the down did when they saw it. I would have liked to hear Pink's remarks to Hiart on the subject of wasting time over useless precautions.

The suitcase was recovered without difficulty. Lex,

however, was not. I could have sworn that I knew where I put him, but every time I went confidently up to him, he either got up and turned out to be a sheep, or lay still and was a patch of dead weeds. There was no time to lose, for we had to be out of the neighbourhood before police got busy on the down and the two roads – and very busy they would be.

'We'll have to leave him,' I insisted at last. 'What does he know?'

'Enough to recognize us both and swear to anything Heyne-Hassingham tells him.'

Well, we found him in the end. The silly blighter had partly recovered from the drug, walked a hundred yards or so, and tumbled down to sleep again by the stream. He came round when we lifted his slack body and shook it.

'It's all right,' I encouraged him. 'You're out of trouble now, you know.'

He replied vaguely that he was very tired. Even with one of us on each side of him, he was too comatose to walk. He kept on grabbing at his bag and mumbling about his papers.

'How soon can you get your car?' Sandorski asked.

'Not enough time. The road may be watched in half an hour. Have you got any more in the bottle?'

He had another ampoule. Lex couldn't help seeing him bring out the syringe. He stuttered *No! No!* in a cracked, terrified voice, but his will was completely paralysed. He even held out his arm.

Then began a melancholy procession across the road and up into the hills on the opposite side. I led the way, holding his ankles, and Sandorski followed with his shoulders. We tied his case on to his stomach. It was the only way to carry it.

I had determined to go to my house. I might have found a better refuge – at any rate, for long enough to examine Lex and look at his papers – but it was essential I should go home. I had at once to confess the whole truth to Cecily, or leave the most horrid doubts and worries in her mind as soon as she heard – and, with the morning milk, she would – of the burned car and its unrecognizable driver. I needed the general to back up my story. My future was at stake in a very different way to that which I had feared for the last three weeks.

It was close on dawn when we entered my back gate. I put Sandorski and Lex in the shed at the bottom of the garden, with some brandy and a kerosene stove. Lex had a luxurious overcoat; I hoped that he also had a tough constitution. It had been a cold night for sleeping in the open.

Then I went upstairs and woke Cecily. I pulled the curtains and turned on her bedside light and told her I needed her help and patience.

She started up, with that glow upon her of a woman who loves and is loved. It can't be analysed. I remember parading an opinion in bachelor days that the test of a girl's beauty was what she looked like when she woke up.

A truth, but a shallow truth. The real test is what you think she looks like.

I said that I had a long story to tell her, and that I wanted hot food and blankets for two men in the shed.

'But why the shed?' she asked.

'Until the children go to school. They might talk.'

'Nothing wakes the children,' she smiled. 'They will be fast asleep for another hour. Why not the spare bedroom?'

'Well, it's just possible that the house might be searched. I don't for a moment think it will be.'

'Seriously searched?'

'No. But just a look-around on some excuse.'

'Put them in the roof-space under the gable. It's warm up there. And if they don't move about, but stay over our room—'

'I'm not going to keep them more than a day,' I said.

'You may have to, darling,' she replied, as if she were perfectly accustomed to such a problem.

I never dreamed she could meet the crisis so calmly. She had all the imaginative fears of a mother of young children. Nightmare after nightmare must have been already gathering under the loyalty which was natural to her, and the discipline she imposed on herself.

We had to hurry. My back garden was hidden from the road, but in daylight it was in full view of the low line of the hills.

Sandorski laid Lex down inside the door as unaffectedly as if he had been carrying a parcel.

'Madame,' he said. 'I am proud to have met the husband of such a wife.'

He kissed her hand, and she managed the receiving end like a Grand Duchess. She'd had it kissed innumerable times before, but never in that superb manner.

I put a ladder against the trap-door in the roof, and we hauled Lex up by a rope under his armpits. A mattress, blankets and a hot-water bottle followed. How the children slept through it I can't imagine, but they did.

Meanwhile Cecily was getting tea and eggs ready in the kitchen – not an easy task in the semi-darkness. The lighting of her bedside lamp would pass, but when I had put it out I lit no others. Any evidence of early activity in the house had to be avoided.

In the grey and uncomfortable light of the dining-room I began my story very irresolutely, and made a thorough mess of it. I did not know how far Sandorski would like me to talk of his business, and of course I felt ashamed of that lighthearted shot at Riemann's expansive target.

'Colonel, my lad, tell her everything,' Sandorski insisted. 'Infantry – that's what you are all through! Won't take a gamble. Where would you be now if I hadn't driven your partridges for you, ha?'

'Fast asleep in bed,' I said.

'Yes – with a damn bad conscience. And this lovely golden madonna of yours wondering what the devil had given you indigestion for the last fortnight. You should be grateful to me.'

'*I* am,' said Cecily.

'If you can still tell me that this evening, Mrs Taine, I will believe in marriage.'

'But you do.'

She gave him a long look, the meaning of which I did not appreciate until she suddenly laid her hand on his.

'My children were the age of yours,' he said. 'They, too, slept well.'

He put his head in his hands. It had been a hard night.

'Go on,' Cecily ordered me quietly.

She was right. My story gave him time to recover. The grey day grew reluctantly. It was a winter dawn, not autumn.

When I had finished, Cecily looked very drawn and stern. She felt strongly that running about the downs with Polish generals in the middle of the night was not one of the duties of the father of a family. I had implied as much ten times over, and pointed out that there was no phase of the action at which I could possibly have extricated myself. I don't think she agreed. There had, perhaps, been a little too much gusto in my account of the night's doings, and not enough repentance.

However, she turned on Sandorski.

'If you are going to stay here, General,' she said, 'you must promise me one thing.'

'Anything,' he answered gallantly.

'You must promise me that no harm shall come to the man you brought with you.'

'My word of honour that no harm shall come to him under your roof,' he replied.

'I didn't say anything about my roof. He's had enough, and you are not to do him any harm at all, now or afterwards.'

'The devil! I don't even know what he's been up to.'

'Nor do I. Or care.'

'But, Mrs Taine, you wouldn't prevent me from sitting on his head if the police were below?'

'I didn't mean that at all, and you know it,' she answered violently.

Sandorski thought for a few seconds. He took his word of honour so seriously that he had to draw up a sort of mental contract.

'I promise,' he said, 'that he shall not be killed or tortured or handed over to anyone but the British police by me or by my order. Will that do?'

'Yes,' she said, and added illogically, 'but I never even thought of such beastly things.'

After breakfast Cecily went up to the roof with the general and took Lex's pulse and temperature. He wasn't cold or shivering, and there didn't seem to be anything wrong with him. Sandorski said he ought to sleep for a few hours more. His first injection had been a stab in the dark. The second was carefully placed.

When the general had been settled in the loft with his patient, I gave him a rope for his future movements, took down the ladder, washed it and put it away. Then I went to bed, pretending the touch of 'flu that I had warned my clerk I was going to have, and Cecily woke the children. Before she gave them breakfast she ran races with them – to get them warm, she said – through the back gate and across the meadow. That effectively destroyed the heavy tracks of Sandorski and myself. Then she carefully examined the shed at the bottom of the garden and removed all traces of occupation.

I didn't expect the police till the evening at earliest. I thought it would take them some time to make the connection between Blossom's land and the burnt car. But when I was about to get up and start the examination of Lex's suitcase with Sandorski, our local constable and his inspector called – in the hope of catching me before I left for the office. Cecily received them downstairs. She was just taking the children to school. The inspector had more low cunning than I ever put to his credit. He chatted with the boys, and quickly found out that Daddy hadn't felt very well the night before and was still in bed. Cecily told me afterwards that the little innocents were so sorry for me, and so convincing, that she almost believed in my illness herself.

The two policemen came up to my room, apologizing profusely. They didn't tell me what had happened. They said that another abandoned vehicle had been found on the upper road. I started to complain, with the querulousness of an invalid, that I had locked my garage at the usual hour and that I didn't see why I should be bothered for parking without lights if somebody pinched my car.

'Oh, it's not that, sir!' the inspector laughed. 'Now, we understand from Mr Blossom that you have rented the shooting over his land. Have you ever noticed anything peculiar up there?'

'I haven't. But, good Lord, Blossom is there all the time! He could tell you better than I.'

'He sent us to you, Mr Taine. He was always busy, he said, but you had your eyes open.'

Then, ruling me, I think, off his list of possible suspects, he came clean. He told me that a burnt car had been found with the body of an unknown male in it, that the police had had a report of the light of an aircraft being seen on Blossom's down, and that they had searched the down at first light, and seen tracks of landing wheels. Had I ever noticed anything which might Lead Me To Believe ...?

Well, no, I hadn't.

'Are you ever up there at night, Mr Taine?'

'No, of course not,' I answered rather too sharply.

'Have you ever seen any sign of poachers?'

I disliked that line of questioning, but what he was after was to get at the names of possible poachers who might have been out at night, and might have noticed something.

At last they went away, leaving me gently sweating under my dressing-gown. It must be a nuisance for the police that almost every man feels slightly guilty in their presence. If that weren't so, it would be much easier for them to pick out the truly guilty.

It was convenient, however, to have the police out of the way at so early an hour. I rapped on the trap-door with a fishing-rod, as a signal for Sandorski to lower his rope and come down. He brought with him Lex's keys. We opened his suitcase.

It was of expensive leather, beautifully fitted inside, and contained everything the painfully well-dressed man would require for the night – silk pyjamas, silk dressing-gown, liver salts in a silver-topped bottle, mono-grammed hair brushes and a deliberately masculine smell. At the bottom, under a change of tasty socks and under-clothing, was a brief-case.

It was a case of thin, imitation, black leather, untidily stuffed with papers. The lock, however, was good – not at all the bit of cheap metal which can be bent out with a wrench of the fingers. I didn't like that case; it seemed to me incongruous. I don't claim any instinct, or any particu-lar powers of observation; but I do believe that you can't live through five years of very active service without devel-oping a strong sense of self-preservation. The night's work had put me back in the old mood of treating unknown objects, whether a pin-up picture, a water-closet plug or a bottle of wine, with extreme care. I don't know how many times I have lectured troops on not whooping with joy every time they came across attractive little surprises.

Sandorski chose a key, but it didn't fit. He was turning the key-ring for another when I picked up the brief-ease and felt it.

'Do you really think this was what they hired a plane for?' I asked.

'Eh? Of course!'

He stretched out his hand for the case, but I didn't offer it.

'Why couldn't they have needed a plane just for Lex?'

'For Lex? They could get him in with a lot less trouble. Documents – these and whatever comes after and the replies – that's what they need an air service for.'

I wanted to be assured that the beastly case was really important. I was not at all eager to prove what I suspected unless it had to be done.

'All right,' I said. 'But this time it's going to be infantry tactics.'

I went into the bathroom (taking the case with me, for I wasn't going to trust the impetuous Sandorski alone with it) and came back with a new razor blade. I held the top of the case firmly and cut the seam which fastened the expanding pleats at the bottom to the stiffer side. The case was filled with loose paper, which I pulled out and Sandorski carefully preserved.

Meanwhile I could feel under my left hand a hard cylinder, apparently attached to the side of the case. That confirmed my suspicion that there was a device of some sort connected to the lock – almost certainly a simple incendiary. I would have liked to take the whole thing out into the garden, but appearance in the garden was taboo. And, anyway, the thing hypnotized me into avoiding all movement. So I started to worry about the new bedroom carpet, which was a convenient and handy object for worry.

When I had cleared the paper I looked inside. The cylinder was an ordinary cardboard roll – the sort that one uses as a container for maps or blue-prints. It was tied over the open ends with tape and sealed with a lead seal. Fingers rather than eyes found a wire running through the tape into the centre of the cylinder and attached to the latch of the case. It looked as if slipping the catch or removing the roll would pull the wire.

I tried to remember, among all the debris of long-forgotten courses on everything from control of flies to detection of wooden mines (the answer in both cases being that you couldn't) what I had learned about all the dirty tricks of sappers. There was something about a spring which released a plunger which broke a vessel of sulphuric acid which did pretty well anything you wanted it to do.

Well, if the pulling of the catch pulled the wire – as it obviously did – and released the plunger, there must be some way by which Lex could prevent it happening. I wished I had done a course on bomb disposal. I wished I had been in the garden. I wished above all that I had the power to take my left hand off the top of the case and that I wouldn't press so hard. I wished that we hadn't bought a new bedroom carpet.

I poked about inside the other end of the cylinder and, sure enough, I found a metal slide with a small knob on the end lying along the cardboard. Lex could have got at this knob from the outside of the case by thrusting a finger into the cheap, pliable material and feeling for it. He couldn't possibly have pulled it; so I put an overcoat over my face, in case I was wrong, and pressed it. It slid home with a comforting click.

There were probably no other risks, but I wasn't going to find out. I cut the stitches that held the cardboard roll to the side of the case, cut the tape, and slipped off the roll. Inside was a metal cylinder, rather larger than a fat fountain pen, still attached by its plunger wire to the interior of the latch. So far as I was concerned, it could stay attached.

I gave Sandorski full marks as a commanding officer. He had made none of his staccato and intelligent suggestions, and had remained perfectly quiet, confident and close to me through the whole business.

We withdrew the papers from their container and unrolled them. They were important enough to justify the extreme precautions that senders and recipients had taken, and for Sandorski they completed the picture. I forget the exact words he used, but his explanation left me with an image of a cone made, let us say, of separate wires, within which he stood. He knew already the circular base of the cone and varying lengths of the upward course of the wires. What these documents gave him was the apex where they all met. We had:

(1) List of cover names.

This was without heading or remark, and was a fairly harmless document if kept apart from the others. It gave us the national leaders who were in correspondence with each other. I can't say they were very impressive, but they had this in common, according to Sandorski: that they were sincere.

(2) Files of leading fascists who were still at large in Italy, Germany and the free countries of Europe, with notes on their reliability.

(3) Propaganda directive for Heyne-Hassingham, with unintelligible code references which looked like dates for action.

(4) A letter to Hiart asking for a report on the family connections, political sympathies and past of certain financiers in Sweden and America, who had offered money.

(5) Draft of an agreement for either signature or initialling by Heyne-Hassingham.

There it was, all the old stuff of the 1930s in a brand new dress! A revolution of the little man to answer the revolution of the littler man. There were to be simultaneous *coups d'état* in the states of Western Europe, and the immediate promise of peace and unity; and until that millennium arrived, all the weapons of communism were to be used to defeat communism. For me and my like it merely meant that the flag over our concentration camp would be white instead of red.

The strength of the movement was in Hiart and his opposite numbers abroad. Since these officials were the most trusted servants of state, the damage they could do by collaborating with each other behind the backs of their governments was incalculable. None of the political chiefs expected anything spectacular of Heyne-Hassingham; but, even so, they had fallen into Ribbentrop's mistake. They thought that his precious People's Union could make such a nuisance of itself that British policy would be forced to be neutral.

'That's the end of Heyne-Hassingham,' I said. Now we go straight to the police.'

'Do we? Colonel, my lad, the value of all this just depends on my reliability and yours.'

'I don't see it.'

'Don't you – ha? Your security people get this sort of thing once a week. Wild political accusations. Just what you'd expect from a bunch of unemployed Polish officers who wanted money. I might have forged all this – easily.'

Up to then I had followed his lead blindly, for I was in such a mess that there was nothing else I could do; but now my responsibility, my duty, had become equal to his.

'No complications,' I said, 'I insist on immediate action.'

He went all general and treated me as if I had been some Polish officer who dared to question his patriotism. I didn't mind. I knew he was loosing off the accumulated strain of the last hour. He told me – if it can be called telling – that because he was anti-communist, it didn't mean he was a pro-fascist traitor.

'Patience, not politics!' he shouted at me. 'Do you understand? Patience is what we need.'

'We do,' I said drily.

He barked at me and fumed and fretted for a moment, trying, for the sake of his pride, to work up his temper again. It couldn't be done. He apologized with a most wholehearted grace. His words were so gallant that they might have been addressed to a woman. The art of the apology has been lost in countries where the duel is out of fashion.

'I'll get off to London tonight,' he said, 'and take Lex with me.'

'Will he go?'

'Go? Why not? Doesn't know where he is. Doesn't know who I am. What can he do? Shove his head out of the window and howl for Heyne-Hassingham? Lex will come like a lamb so long as we don't frighten him. Look the blighter up!'

We found Lex on the list of cover names. Sandorski knew of him, but they had never met. He was a Czech of Austrian descent, and had been, in better days, a prominent lawyer with a taste for wild-cat politics. We also found Pink's true name. He was the tough and eccentric son of an obscure English peer, and he had been fired out of the Navy for gross insubordination. Evidently he had been under the impression that he was Nelson.

Peter Sandorski boldly made his arrangements by telephone. There was no reason to suppose we were under any suspicion, and indeed at that time – which was about midday – we were not. He called a Whitehall number and spoke to a friend named Roland, asking him to make arrangements for two air passages to Vienna and for a safe – he stressed safe – lodging meanwhile. It was clear that he had the connections to travel freely, even semi-officially. How far the secret services of Western powers supplied him with funds, I do not know; but his organization of Poles and expatriates, playing for European peace and stability, must have been extremely useful.

When Cecily came back from her shopping and her children, she gave us a picnic lunch in the roof, and herself kept watch below. Lex returned to consciousness and gave little trouble. I think it was Cecily who put confidence into him. He couldn't believe that such a woman would feed him and fuss over him if anything were intended against his life or liberty. As an experienced lawyer he must have been a fair judge of human nature. What he made of us then, I don't know. He probably trusted us provisionally, failing anyone else to trust. We told him that his suitcase was in a safe place, and lent him a razor. We also gave him a good story to the effect that we had had to drug him, so that if he were caught he wouldn't be able to talk until Heyne-Hassingham had an opportunity to tell him what to say.

Our plan was simple, and I imagine it would have worked. I was going to sneak Sandorski and Lex into the garage after dark – which could be done provided my house was not watched at very close range – make them lie in the bottom of the car till we were clear of the immediate neighbourhood, and then drive them to a bus stop. I couldn't drive them far, in case there was a police cordon round the district; if we were stopped and questioned, Lex, who spoke with a strong foreign accent and had no identity documents, would put the lot of us under suspicion. On a country bus, however, and then a train to London, it was certain they would pass through as any other citizens.

The children came back from school, and Cecily arranged to walk up to the village with them on an ice-cream expedition in order to get them out of the way while Sandorski and Lex descended from the roof. It was growing dark and she was just about to start, when we had another call from the inspector of police.

'We have been checking the footprints on Mr Blossom's land, sir,' he said after some polite preliminaries, 'and we would like to get clear the people who had every right to be there. Would you mind showing me your shooting boots?'

Fortunately I had cleaned them. He took the measurements and a note of missing studs on the sole. He looked puzzled, but preserved a beautiful mask of official cordiality.

'When were you last at the northern end of the down?'

'Let me see,' I said. 'Where exactly do you mean?'

'A little east of the curve of the valley. There's a big holly bush half-way down, if you remember.'

'I know. I was there last Saturday.'

'Not later?'

'No, Inspector.'

He was on to something, but I wasn't worried. I felt quite certain that the short, springy turf wouldn't reveal a measurable footprint, and certainly not the time when it was made.

'Mr Taine,' he said. 'Suppose I were to tell you that I had good reason to believe you were on the down some time yesterday or last night?'

'My dear man, my wife and children have already told you that I was in bed with a touch of 'flu. And all yesterday I was in the office, and there are dozens of people to prove it. May I ask why you think I wasn't, or wouldn't it be professional?'

'I don't see why you shouldn't know,' he answered. 'I have two sets of prints, apparently yours, in wet cow dung. Now can you help me, Mr Taine? We know perfectly well that your life is an open book and that you don't run secret aircraft.'

Possibly I should have helped him. On the other hand, I didn't feel like explaining to my local inspector that I had first killed, then buried, then burnt an unknown male. That kind of thing was obviously better handled, if it ever had to come out at all, on a high level, between Sandorski and his friend Roland.

'Well, but look here – how long does wet cow dung take to dry in damp weather? Surely that is a bit beyond the country police?'

'It's beyond me, Mr Taine,' he laughed. 'But we've got

some assistance from Scotland Yard on this case – and better still.'

I said that I didn't know there was anything better than Scotland Yard.

He told me. After all, he was dead certain that I was innocent; and I was a respectable neighbour, entitled, after all this trouble, to a bit of thrilling and confidential gossip.

'There's a gentleman staying with Mr Robert Heyne-Hassingham. Catches spies, and all that. *You* know. Well, Mr Taine, if you don't mind my taking your boots away with me, I'm sure they'll find that those prints were made on Saturday. Maybe Scotland Yard knows more about bulls than cows. Ha, ha!'

'Ha, Ha!' I answered dutifully.

'And meanwhile, Mr Taine – just as a matter of form – I'm afraid I must ask you to be at home or at the office tomorrow. And I'll bring you a statement to sign in the morning.'

When he had gone I got Sandorski down at once from the roof.

'Peter,' I said, 'there was a policeman here. It will take him twenty minutes to get back to county headquarters, and about ten minutes after that Hiart will know it was me. Now what?'

He opened a rapid fire of questions and got the position clear.

'Hiart is trying an impossible bluff,' I insisted. 'I have only to produce those documents, and you to back me up.'

'Colonel, my lad, Sandorski forged them. Sandorski told you a yarn. Sandorski got you to help him land a plane. Sandorski and you murdered the man who came in it. Can you prove that isn't true?'

'The beacons,' I said.

'My lad, they used gloves, and we were in a hurry and didn't.'

'Lex, then.'

'Hiart thinks Lex is dead. He'll get a shock when he finds he isn't. But he'll manage to have a word with him before the police.'

'But Hiart and Pink and his chaps. We heard them and saw them,' I protested.

'Indeed you did. And they nearly caught you and me in the act of landing that plane.'

'But it's a nightmare.'

'I've never put the blame on the staff,' he said, 'and I'm not going to start now. I'll keep you out of it.'

I didn't like the idea of surrender, and I told him so.

'Too many non-combatants about,' he replied, nodding his head towards the uproarious noise that was coming from the living-room. 'They have no business in this sort of thing.'

'I'm going to give 'em a better world than this even if I go to gaol for it.'

'Ten minutes of your better world is up,' he said.

'I can't help feeling Lex is the key.'

'Produce him to the police, you think?'

'It's bound to rattle Hiart.'

'For a moment, until he can get a word with him. Then all Lex has to say is the truth – ha? – that we did receive him, and that Hiart tried to get him away.'

Sandorski shot out a hand to me for silence. His left eye sparkled with life, showing up the artificial right in fierce contrast that I had never noticed before.

'Lex!' he said. 'Quick!'

He did the rope trick into the roof, with me after him.

'Lex, if we can get you away from here, where do you go?'

He used Lex's real name, which I needn't repeat. That gave the man confidence.

'Where I go? Why?'

'The police are on to us. But there's still a chance of delivering your bag. Where were you to go if the plane made a forced landing?'

'Why don't you know?' Lex replied stolidly.

'Because my orders were to take you here. But it's bust open, my lad. It's hot. We've got to get out.'

Lex thought it over and decided to trust us.

'Flat 9, 26, Fulham Park Avenue, London.'

'Who do you ask for?'

'I think empty. I have keys.'

'Get a stiff needle and black thread from your missus.' Sandorski ordered me. 'And tell her to hop it now with the children.'

'What's the idea?'

'Bolt. Skip. Now – ha? If we can get Lex to London, we'll beat 'em yet.'

I left Sandorski to tidy up the roof space; he hadn't time to hide all traces of occupation, but he hoped to indicate that only one man had been there, not two.

'Go out now with the children, my darling,' I said to Cecily, 'and get them that ice-cream. When you come back we shan't be here. But Hiart will be, and the police. They are bound to find out that someone was in the roof, but say you know nothing about it. Say I was certainly behaving oddly, but stick to your story that I never went out last night. When you took the children to the village, I said I would follow you in a minute, and we'd have a quick one at the local: Got it?'

'But where will I be able to find you?' she cried.

'Safe as can be. In the hands of the police. But I don't want to be caught till we've sunk this People's Union for good and all.'

Our parting wasn't as sentimental as either of us would have liked, but one gets used to that in a family. The children were exasperating. They were deep in a game and decided that they didn't want ice-cream. They wouldn't put on their coats. A hat couldn't be found. And all the time the precious minutes were ticking away. My last view of George was of the little scamp dragging back on Cecily's firm hand, and howling loudly.

I turned off all the lights and went out to reconnoitre the garden and the back.

'Careful,' Sandorski suggested.

'What the hell do you think I'm going to be?'

'Right, Colonel, my lad! But just remembered again that Hiart thinks Lex is dead. If you were too, how convenient for him! Don't say he will. Doesn't like violence. But it must occur to him.'

I quietly unlocked the garage door. Lex slipped in, keeping to the shadows, and lay down in the back of the car, where we covered him with a rug and his splendid overcoat. Sandorski threw in the brief-case, wrapped up in a brown paper parcel, and told him what it was. At the last moment he dashed back into the house to cut the telephone wires. I jumped out, too, and locked the garage, so that, if we hadn't been watched, it wouldn't be immediately obvious that my car was out.

It was now 6.15, and exactly half an hour since the inspector had left. We couldn't have more than a minute or two to get away. As a matter of course I turned to the right, up the valley, for I couldn't go the other way in case I ran slap into the police car racing out from Dorchester; but I had barely changed up into top before Sandorski shouted:

'Stop! Damn!'

I thought he had forgotten something essential, and that we were done.

'Straight into the net! Rabbits! Attack, ha? Attack, even if you've got to run! Turn the car round and put out your lights, my lad.'

When I had obeyed, he explained that just as soon as the Yard man and Hiart compared those boots of mine with a plaster cast, they would be pretty sure that I and my companion, if I had one, would try to escape. Any available police would at once be ordered by telephone to keep an eye on the road we were following. The police car itself could stop the other end of the road.

I climbed up the bank to watch. I didn't have long to wait. Indeed the lights of the cars were already in sight. There were two of them. They stopped outside my darkened house. I could hear the police hammering on the door. Then they went round to the back, and the lights were switched on. The cars had left plenty of room on the road. I tore past them, with the needle of the speedometer jumping from twenty to sixty. I was keeping my eyes on the road. Sandorski said that everyone was in the house or at the back, and that the only people to see us were the drivers of the police cars.

I reckoned that one of the drivers would run into the house, that somebody would then jump for the telephone and discover that the wires were cut, and that only then would one of the cars turn and give chase.

That gave me a start of at least one minute, and probably three, and I felt reasonably sure of holding it even against the brilliant driving of the police. I went along that road to my office, by car or bicycle, six days a week, and I knew every twist and narrowing. I decided to stick to it, and not to jam myself in the lanes. A cross-country route might trick the pursuit for an hour or two, but in the end would only give them time to draw the cordon tighter round the district where we must be.

I did the seven miles to the outskirts of Dorchester in eight minutes, and please God I never have to do such a piece of driving again! Sandorski reported nothing in sight behind. At the bottom of the town was a fork, and there I turned sharp left, going back more or less parallel to the road I had come on, and separated from it by flat water meadows.

There I drove sedately like any family farmer returning home. I saw the lights of a fast car hurling along the road we had just left, and gambled that the police would also see my lights, and decide that it couldn't be me. That was what happened. Sandorski reported that the police car had rushed straight on up the hill into Dorchester. There they were bound, as they thought, to have news of me. I must have been seen or stopped.

Now we sailed away northwards over the downs, passing little traffic and, thank heavens, no village bobby to notice our number. Not that he need bother with numbers. My car was a smart light grey, and horribly conspicuous at night.

When I thought we were likely to have passed out of the probable area of search, I turned into a lane and stopped. Far beyond us, of course, there would be checkpoints or roving patrol cars to cut us off from London, but we were now between the lines with time to think.

I told Lex to come up and take a breather. He put out an unhappy and disgusting head.

'I vos ill,' he said.

'All for the cause!' exclaimed Sandorski. 'Heil Hitler!'

'Why you say that?' asked Lex very seriously.

'Ask our friend here, my lad!' Sandorski said with an air of triumphant mystery.

'He is then alive?'

'Go and wash your face,' I said. 'I can hear a stream down there to the right somewhere.'

I had grabbed a bottle of rum as last-minute baggage, and when Lex had gone we had a couple.

'One thing I didn't have time to tell you,' the general remarked. 'Mustn't use our names before this chap.'

'I haven't, I think. Nor you – except that you will call me Colonel. But that's all right, as nobody else does.'

'We'll make it,' he said.

'We'll want a lot of luck. Do you realize I've got to stop for petrol somewhere?'

'And I've got to telephone.'

'What on earth for?'

'Didn't I tell you?'

'You told me to get out of the house and bring a needle and thread.'

'That's to sew up Lex's brief-case,' he explained. 'Must be in decent condition when he delivers it to Heyne-Hassingham.'

'Lord! Can you arrange that?'

'Yes, of course. And room wired for sound. If I ask for a chance to prove my innocence I'll get it. Enough influence for that, ha? But nobody's going to know me if I get arrested. Why should they? Might be guilty. I'm not trusted. I'm just a source of information.'

It was a wild scheme, but I could see that if we could deliver Lex to that flat at 26, Fulham Park Avenue, it might succeed. It seemed to me, however, that our chance of ever reaching London was slim. In the course of the night the movements of my grey car were certain to be reported by some policeman. On the other hand, to judge by the newspapers, England was full of criminals regularly escaping with stolen cars. I supposed that they were prepared for the game, chose neutral body work, and had handy false number plates such as Hiart himself used.

The telephoning had to be tackled as soon as possible before the description of me and my car had been circulated too widely. It was improbable, we thought, that the police had any description of Sandorski or even his name. Hiart wouldn't tell them, for he couldn't be sure that Sandorski was in England at all, and he was not likely to commit himself when he didn't know what questions he would have to meet. Though he held a possible winning hand, he must be just as alarmed as we were. It was a comforting thought. About the only one available.

Lex came back from the stream, pale and dirty, but looking slightly more like a travelling lawyer than a criminal. I drove on, steering a slow and uncertain course through the by-roads. I was trying to find a safe route round Salis-bury, well to the north of it.

We crossed the main road to London between Sher-borne and Shaftesbury, using quite unnecessary caution. Half a mile further on, running through Hinton FitzPaine, we saw a telephone kiosk just clear of the last houses. It seemed to be as remote as any, so I drove up a stony little lane, where there was certain to be no traffic at that time of night, and where we could safely wait while Sandorski went into the village.

I could not go with him. Lex was the difficulty. We couldn't very well walk off with the brown paper parcel for which he was responsible. On the other hand, we didn't want to leave him alone with it. So I had to stay.

'Have you got enough small change?' I yelled after the general.

He was doubtful, so I emptied my trouser pocket into his. There was a fair supply of shillings and sixpences and coppers, enough for a couple of trunk calls to London, especially as it was only eight o'clock, and he would get the cheap evening tariff.

I sat there for half an hour talking to Lex. He was a lot more likeable than his ideas – a solemn and mistak-en crusader, but definitely a crusader. Even war and the law courts hadn't cured him of a boyish sense of romance. He still believed that – possibly with himself as chancel-lor – a despotism could be benevolent. So, I suppose, did Heyne-Hassingham, on condition that he was the despot.

When I heard Sandorski stamping up the lane I was already beginning to get anxious. I nipped out of the car to meet him. He was quivering with nerves and temper. Even his footsteps were dancing and angry like those of a vicious horse.

'Gone to the club!' he informed me in a sort of stifled scream.

Then he imitated the voice of the telephone operator, and I thought he would burst his arteries.

'Another one and tuppence, please. Damn their one and tuppences! Damn! Damn! Damn! Got his office building. Six blasted minutes before some ... can tell me he's out. Cut off twice. Had to use another one and tuppence to get back. What message did he leave? At the club. Got the bloody club. Porter couldn't find him. Put another sixpence in the box, please. I hadn't got another sixpence. Colonel, I will not try again. It is the end!'

'Here, let me have a go!' I said. 'I'll come with you.'

'How do we get change?'

'At the pub, of course.'

'What about that?' – he nodded towards Lex. 'Or have you cut his puking, blasted throat before the ... hangman breaks it?'

'That governess of yours was a remarkable woman,' I said.

'... my governess!'

'I wouldn't put it past you. Now listen, Peter. Lex is nearly asleep. Patience!'

I got him back into the car.

'We have to wait an hour,' I said to Lex. 'And there's nothing to do. So why not relax?'

I suppose the next ten minutes must have been as exasperating as any in the general's whole life. I made him pretend to settle down to sleep. It wasn't a very good pretence. Every muscle in his body was tight, and his occasional snorts sounded more like temper than repose. I myself kept up the air of tranquillity so determinedly that I actually dozed, and was awoken by a savage dig from Sandorski.

It was quarter to nine. Lex, bruised, worn out and still dopey, was fast asleep. We extracted the brown paper parcel and ran down into Hinton FitzPaine.

I went into the pub and called for a rum – since it was what I had been drinking – and offered a note in payment. Of course I got three half crowns which were no good for the slots in the telephone box. I ordered another drink – for I didn't want to ask outright for shillings and sixpences in case someone guessed I wanted them for a telephone – and in my eagerness to attract the attention of the landlord pushed further into the room.

It was the foulest piece of bad luck, equal to all that careless and insanitary cow had brought on me. I ran into the county surveyor who was having a quick one on his way home from the inspection of some miserable local drainage scheme.

'Well, if it isn't Roger Taine!' he roared, exploding my

name from the smoke around the darts board.

I hoped the local policeman wasn't in the bar. No one else, I thought, could know I was wanted till the morning papers. Nevertheless, I watched the room rather than the surveyor, and met the fixed stare of a man sitting on the settle along the opposite wall. He composed his face and looked away with a slight flush. He was a bad actor; but I doubt if I, in the horrified surprise of hearing my name, was any better.

My confounded friend shoved his way round the table towards me. I told him that I was in a desperate hurry, but I had to have a drink with him. I was sure that Sandorski, in his present mood of reckless impatience would come storming into the bar if I kept him waiting long.

The man on the settle waited a minute and then got up and passed the length of the bar, saying casually and rather loudly to the landlord that he was going to call his wife. The telephone was out of sight, on the wall of the passage that led out to the scullery and the beer barrels.

'I'm sure I know that man,' I said to the landlord. I didn't, of course, and didn't want to. He was a type I don't care for – worn and frustrated and keeping up a smart, grey moustache to compensate for his general air of genteel futility.

'Likely you would, sir. He keeps the filling station and café on the main road. Looks like Aladdin's cave in the pantomime, though it wants a bit of paint and plaster, as who doesn't? Teddy Bear's Picnic he calls it, 'cos 'is name is

Edward Bear. Ah, 'e's a one, 'e is! Ever heard of the People's Union?'

'Why, let me see ...'

'Didn't think you would 'ave! But we *has* to hear of it. Mr Bear is the county secretary, he is. I don't allow no politics in 'ere. Still, his People's Union don't 'ardly count as politics. More like one of them last-day religions if you ask me.'

It wasn't surprising that Hiart had mobilized any of his People's Union stalwarts who might be of use. It was also possible that the police, as a matter of routine, had warned filling stations on the main road. I escaped from the pub while the chorus of approval was going on, and found Sandorski fuming at the corner of the village street.

'I know, but listen!' I said. 'I've been recognized. There's a man who mustn't see a stranger telephoning. I'm going to lead him away. I'll give you ten minutes to finish and get back to the car. Don't be longer.'

I poured a stream of small change into him and hurried up the street again to the pub. I was only just in time to draw the attention of Mr Edward Bear, who was looking for my car. I pretended not to notice him, and walked out of the village in the direction of the main road. He followed, but let the distance between us grow too far. It was a lonely road and pitch dark, and he wasn't used to trailing murderers. Who is? I don't think he had any enthusiasm for the job. It was a bit different from distributing pamphlets.

Where a farm track crossed the road I allowed him to lose me. He made half-hearted darts up the three possible ways I might have gone. Then he stood at the cross-roads, mumbling to himself. The only words I could catch were a pathetically childish *I wish I hadn't*, and later on a stern *Service, Edward, service!*

This was annoying. I had given Sandorski his ten minutes, and the ten lengthened into twenty. I was far too close to the wretched man. I couldn't move. Then it occurred to me that he wasn't waiting in pure indecision, but for somebody's arrival. I did not know what to do. To break cover and bolt was far too compromising.

I heard a car coming down the road. Mr Bear stood in the shaft of light and waved. The car stopped. Inside were Hiart, Pink and a driver. Hiart got out.

'Well, Bear?' he said in his high-pitched voice. 'Well? I thought you were to wait for us at the inn. You must get used to obedience, you know. You're working for the State now, not the Party. Good practice for you!'

I didn't wonder he had specialized in Intelligence. As an officer in command of troops, he would have been shot in the back. This was the rebuke educational. Officers will remember that they command Citizens, and will exercise Patience at All Times. I'd rather have Sandorski at his worst than be shown Patience by Hiart.

'I followed him here,' said Bear sulkily, for he had been expecting praise.

'Here? Here?'

'Yes, here,' said Pink wearily. 'He said here, and I suppose he means here.'

Mr Bear explained rapidly what had happened. He was a tiresome little bundle of pretences, but, if you come to think of it, he had shown a heap of guts.

'Then his car is up one of these two tracks,' said Pink.

'Oh, nonsense!' Hiart exclaimed, his voice leaping to an offensive falsetto on the first syllable. 'You haven't heard a car, Bear, have you? No! Well, if he knew he was followed by you he'd have driven off very fast. And if he didn't know he was followed, he'd have driven off normally. The car isn't here at all. Flash your light on that mud and see!'

It was no wonder that Hiart was disliked. And he was ten times more exasperating because he was always right.

'Taine is probably behind the hedge,' Pink said, 'with a gun trained on you.'

Hiart jumped to the other side of the car.

'I find those remarks in poor taste, Pink,' he complained.

Fortunately Pink didn't test his theory, for I *was* behind the hedge.

Hiart turned to Bear.

'What was he doing in the pub?'

'Having a drink of course,' Pink interrupted impatiently. 'Why not?'

'Nonsense! Nonsense! That's a risk Sandorski would never have allowed.'

'You've got Sandorski on the brain,' Pink answered. 'Taine burned up Lex, and therefore he shot Riemann, and we don't know who put him up to it, because you didn't stop to see. And I rather think Riemann is alive – unless you shot him yourself and know he isn't.'

'Deplorable!' Hiart protested.

There was a certain smug satisfaction in his voice. He evidently liked to be accused of daring deeds.

'Bear, since you have been here, have you heard a car leave the village?'

'No, sir.'

'Then they are still here, and somewhere on the other side of the houses.'

They all got into the car and drove down into the village. I ran after them as close as I dared. They stopped at the pub and went inside – no doubt to find the surveyor and confirm my identity.

In that one street it was difficult to pass the car and its driver. All I could do was to enter the inn yard, go round behind the building and come out again into the open with my back to the car. I walked unsteadily and gave a loud belch of satisfaction as if I were bound homewards from the side door. As soon as I had passed out of the range of the one village light I ran for my car.

Sandorski's mood had changed. He was still on edge – but merely because he couldn't think what had happened to me. Otherwise he was purring with pleasure. He had at last got hold of his friend, Roland, who had promised to prepare the flat at 26, Fulham Park Avenue, forthwith. Roland as yet had heard nothing of our adventures, but had warned the general, on principle, not to wreck all chances of help by getting himself and Lex arrested.

In the silence of the night I heard Hiart's car pull away from the village pub. If I reversed down the lane I should arrive at the corner about the same time as they did. If I stayed where I was, I feared they would have a look at the tempting mouth of the lane and walk far enough up it to find us. The worn and stony surface might or might not reveal the fresh track of tyres, but I had an exaggerated respect for Hiart's hunting instinct; he would spot that lane as just the place to leave a car if you didn't want it to be seen while you went down to the village.

So there was nothing for it but to go on up the hill and pray that we didn't find ourselves in a cul de sac. As we went I tried to tell Sandorski – without very much success – what had happened. For Lex's benefit I called our pursuers the deviationists. At any rate, I made it clear that they were not the police.

The lane was so narrow that I could drive without lights. The hedges on each side brushed the wings, and loose stones crackled and spurted under the wheels. The gradient at the worst places must have been one in four. The noise of our progress in bottom gear attracted Hiart and Pink. Sandorski reported light behind us.

At the top was a stout five-barred gate. The general jumped out and opened it.

'Give me a rendezvous, quick!' he demanded.

'Can't. I don't know where we are.'

'Damn! Wanted to puncture their tyres when they stopped. Pity – ha?'

It was a pity. But we might never have met again, and I didn't know what the drill was if ever we reached London. We went on. The lane ended and we bumped over some sort of grass track. I had to use my lights. They revealed nothing but more grass and ruts.

This was not the sort of situation that suited Sandorski, for we dared not show fight. By one of his favourite rearguard actions we had everything to lose. If Lex were caught and his papers recovered, nothing could save us from the dock – though, I suppose, after months of agony for me and my family, we might have been acquitted. Still better for Hiart and Heyne-Hassingham, was our death. That would be the end of any evidence on what had really happened at my shoot, and Hiart – if he arranged things to prove self-defence and could put his fingers in his ears at the critical moment – would be thanked by the police for his gallant chase.

I came to a cow-trampled mud-hole where the ruts petered out. Beyond the hole were roughly stopped gaps. Both led to cultivated fields. This looked uncommonly like the end. I turned off my lights and got out of the car, waiting to recover my night sight. It was the usual dirty, damp November night. We might have been on some exotic plateau of the Rockies or Andes instead of a hill in populous England four hundred feet above the sea. There wasn't a signal from humanity, except the faint smell of wood smoke drifting up from the village on the south-west wind.

The car behind us had stopped to go through the gate. I heard it shut again behind them. I let them drive on towards me, for the ruts leading into blackness would take their attention away from anything that might be happening in the outer dark. Then I turned my car to face the open grass and shot off into the night like a plane taking off. It sounds dangerous, and it was. On the other hand, one somehow knows, in a countryside that forms part of one's blood, what the sweep of the land is likely to be. I merely mean that I knew I should meet an obstruction before I went over the edge of anything, and that the obstruction would be soft. I also felt sure that I wasn't going to meet anything at all immediately. That may have been due to the feel of the grass or the wind, or, less mysteriously, to rum. One in the car and three more, unwanted, on an empty stomach undoubtedly made my driving optimistic.

We had the devil's own luck. I missed a pond by inches and then went slap through a barbed wire fence into a field of kale. It couldn't have been better. The kale was high enough and formed a dark enough mass for me to begin to brake in time. When we hit it, we merely crashed for a few yards through the soft stalks.

On the damp ploughland it took time to reverse and turn. Lex and Sandorski jumped out to push. I doubt if they made much difference, but I wouldn't like to underrate the sheer nervous will-power of Sandorski in a crisis. What really saved us were the fibrous stumps of the kale, which gave just enough purchase for the back wheels.

When I had pulled out, and back through the gap in the fence, I stopped for the two to get in. Meanwhile Hiart and Pink had followed up the ruts to the mud-hole. There they picked up our tracks in their lights, and came nosing along them. They were now something less than three hundred yards away. They couldn't see us, for the bushes at the edge of the pond I had just missed were partly in the way, and the background and skyline were broken; but undoubtedly they would pick us out as soon as we moved. Sandorski told Lex to lie on the floor, and folded himself into a small tense spring between the dashboard and the front seat.

I started rolling gently over the field towards the lane. The movement, as I feared, attracted attention, and the two great eyes of the following car swivelled round until they were full on my side. They rested there a couple of seconds as Hiart's driver swung round in a quarter circle to keep me in view. Then he quickly turned the full semi-circle and lit up the rolling field ahead.

'He's going for the gate!' yelled Sandorski.

Of course he was. I might have betted Hiart would think of that. Once he had his car across the gate or in the lane, there was no way out for us except on foot. We might have tried it, I suppose, and played another successful hide-and-seek in the darkness, but dawn and the police and dogs would soon have settled us.

My course into the kale had taken me more or less di-agonally across this great field or down. I now had to run parallel to its lower boundary in order to reach the gate, and at some time I had to swing well out into the field in order to go through. What the boundary was, I don't know. The thick black shadows looked like a young plan-tation. At any rate, it was something impassable to cars, and I had it looming fifty yards to my left. To my right and about two hundred yards away was Hiart's car. I call it Hiart's, but remembering this moment of violence I am sure Pink had taken command, and that he was thinking in terms of naval engagement.

On went my headlights. They showed good grass ahead, and I pulled up level. For a second or two we were racing on lines not quite parallel that would intersect at the gate. Then our courses rapidly converged. I couldn't avoid it. I was driving along the obstruction to my left, and it was curving and forcing me closer to Pink.

I had one vast advantage over Pink's driver. I was run-ning for my life, and he wasn't. A split second before I got jammed against the edge of the plantation, I braked hard and passed behind them and took the outer berth. My car had terrific acceleration in second, and I pulled up level again at the cost of two leaves of a spring. There weren't more than twenty yards between us, and Pink took a shot at me. I think it must have been meant for the tyre, for he would find it hard to satisfy the police that a shot at obvious fugitives was in self-defence. It went through the rear window and nearly got Lex, who was being tossed under his coat from floor to air and back again. It was a good bit of gunnery from one moving car to another. He was only three feet high and left.

I don't suppose we ever went much above thirty miles an hour, but over that surface the speed was as alarming as eighty on a bad road. I closed in on them from the outside in order to wreck the driver's nerves and force him into the plantation I had just escaped. Then I heard Pink's quarterdeck voice:

'Ram him Jimmy!'

The driver must have been a naval man too. His quick response was worthy of the service. I turned away and skidded, and he just touched my back bumper. I heard Pink open up with his forward turret. This time he only scored the number plate and a ricochet off the wing which starred my driving window and frightened me into an extra burst of speed.

Pink was so pleased to have something to shoot at, that he stayed on my tail a second too long. He allowed me to get so far out into the field that I could go for the gate. If he had raced straight for the objective, he would have had his car across it before I could complete my turn.

I could distinguish the gate now. It was shut. I've seen a galloping horse miss his jump and shatter a five-barred gate without breaking his legs. I prayed that my car would do the same and roared straight at it. Pink, too late, cut across behind. He was only three or four lengths away, and it seemed certain that this time he must ram me broadside on before I could be through. By how much he missed me I don't know. There was a crash and a lot of flying wood; then another crash as Pink's car hurtled into the hedge; and I found myself shooting down the lane, fighting to control the car as it bounced from one bank to the other.

Near the bottom of the lane I slithered and scraped to a stop, and told Sandorski that we were out. He uncurled himself and straightened painfully into the front seat. Lex remained groaning and muttering in the bottom of the car. I began to feel sorry for the poor man. Ever since we had picked him up, he had had the life of a sack of potatoes going to market.

'What happened?' the general asked.

I told him that the deviationists were in the middle of a hedge and probably upside down, that we had a minute or two at least before they could disentangle themselves, and that I'd explain it all later. The question now was: should we turn left at the bottom of the lane into the unknown, or right and up to the main road through Hinton FitzPaine?

'How many people were there in the car?' he asked.

'The two you know and the driver.'

'Not the man you call Teddy Bear?'

'No.'

'Then they left him behind to telephone the police.'

'If he did, we're mighty near the end,' I said. 'One of

the springs is on its last legs, and we must be nearly out of petrol.'

He bounced into the lane and beckoned me to join him where Lex could not hear what we said.

'Why not telephone for a car?' he suggested.

'And some oysters, too.'

'Hadn't thought of it! Just what we need! But would the Teddy Bear's Picnic have oysters?'

'Meat loaf,' I said. 'Pig's lung and soya bean. Ministry of Food Special. What the hell are you talking about?'

'Telephoning for a car, Colonel, my lad. Mr Heyne-Hassingham's secretary speaking – ha? Hiart's car smashed up. Wants another to take him to London at once. Heil People's Union. Off we go! Why not?'

I looked at my watch and shook it. It was working all right. What I couldn't believe was that only some fourteen minutes had passed since I rejoined Sandorski and started up the lane. Still, it was enough for a patrol car to have arrived, if one was coming at all.

'Isn't it possible that Hiart saw his chance to settle accounts with us alone?' I asked. 'It would be a godsend to him if he could keep the police out of it. Suppose he just sent Bear home to stand by for orders?'

'Home? Pub after all that excitement! I'll get him out of it. It's a bloody awful gamble. Come on!'

We drove hard through the village, seeing no one on the way, and stopped a little distance up one of the tracks at that cross where Bear had met Hiart and Pink. Sandorski jumped out and ran back to Hinton FitzPaine.

He went straight to the pub and hauled out Bear, who of course didn't know him and had no description of him. It was touch and go, for at any moment somebody from the wrecked car might be down in the village. Bear didn't hesitate. He couldn't possibly doubt any man who knew as much about his recent movements as Sandorski did; and I expect he remembered. Hiart's remarks on getting used to obedience.

They came striding past the cross-roads, with Bear chattering away in a state of tremendous excitement. I cleared my car of all possessions and followed with Lex at a reasonable distance. We walked along the main road until Teddy Bear's Picnic came in view. Then I parked Lex behind a tree and went forward to reconnoitre. I had his brown paper parcel. He was no longer worrying about it. He had resigned all responsibility into our hands.

Teddy Bear's Picnic consisted of three loathsome arches facing the petrol pumps and the main road. It had pleased Mr Bear and his builder to disguise the nakedness of con-crete with a vast thickness of plaster decoration – now cracked – representing boughs, wattle and odd chunks of rock. The right-hand arch contained the café, and the left the office. Both were closed. The doors of the centre arch were open, and the blaze of light revealed a too ambitious and untidy workshop, with Mr Bear pouring oil into a six-seater limousine.

Sandorski was strolling up and down the road, giving

an excellent imitation of an important and impatient politician. He was keeping a careful watch on the hedgerow, and when I waved a handkerchief he came over and whispered the news.

It was good and bad. Hiart's driver had telephoned the garage for a car and had been answered, after much delay, by Mrs Bear. That put our bona fides beyond a doubt. But it was a safe assumption that he had also telephoned the police, so that a patrol car could be expected very shortly.

The driver must have been in the telephone box when Sandorski and Bear came out of the pub. He had left it to Mrs Bear to get hold of her husband. We couldn't understand why he had been in such an unthinking hurry. The explanation – as we found out afterwards – was that Pink and Hiart were both hurt, Hiart badly, and the driver didn't want to leave them alone at the mercy of a desperado who might return any minute.

I was hesitant about car stealing and knocking out Bear. Even if we were eventually proved innocent of major crimes, the police couldn't overlook gangsterism of that sort.

'People's Union require me to drive!' Sandorski assured me. 'And People's Union pay cash down for hire. Where's the stealing?'

'You can get away with that?'

'Why not – ha? Shan't we want good men at the People's Ministry of Transport? Ruthless men like Bear! Obeying orders without question! Nip up the road with Lex and bundle in when I come abreast of you.'

'How are you going to account for starting out the wrong way?'

'Pick up a parcel!' he snorted. 'Chaps who want reasons for everything don't join the People's Union.'

Sandorski kept Bear occupied while we sneaked past the garage along the grass verge of the road. Lights came tearing towards us, and I shoved Lex down in the ditch and joined him. A black saloon whistled smoothly past us, and I saw inside it the peaked caps of the police. We hadn't much time – perhaps five minutes before the cops joined Hiart and Pink at the top of the lane, and anything up to quarter of an hour before somebody got on to Bear to find out why the car hadn't arrived. Meanwhile the alarm would go out for my grey car, or, if they found it, for a man or men on foot. Twenty miles to Salisbury. We might just have time to reach the town before the make and number of our limousine reached the patrol cars and the constables on point duty.

When I had experienced a few minutes of Sandorski's driving I had no doubt that we should make Salisbury if we didn't die horribly first. He seemed to forget that the English rule of the road was the left, or perhaps he was merely holding the middle at all costs. When I protested, he had the ignorance to say that he was a damn sight safer than I was. It was not true. I am a most careful driver. I resented it very strongly.

Salisbury streets were comforting, and not only because at last I could relax. The pubs were just closing. There were people about, people with whom we could mix, among whom we could be lost. We were plain citizens, not outlaws, for the moment; but it would be a short moment.

'Where to?' the general asked.

I directed him out of the centre into quiet residential streets. A dark house with a longish drive looked tempting. We ran the car into the drive, turned off the lights, and left it. That was a good choice. We could count on all the car parks and streets being searched immediately; but in a private garden we were safe until the owner discovered our car next morning. And if he were out and returned that night, he would probably be content to curse the impudence of unknown persons for parking in his drive.

What to do now? Sandorski was all for stealing a car, but I wouldn't have it. Hiring was too dangerous, for the police would certainly do the round of garages. Hitch-hiking? Well, if Sandorski and I had been alone, we might have tried to stop a friendly lorry-driver on the outskirts of the town. But Lex was nearly finished – so done that we desperately considered putting him in a hotel and hiding ourselves wherever we could. Lex kept on saying he was sorry, but that he wasn't used to such exertion. Again I found myself liking the man. He might fairly have blamed us for using drugs on him, but he didn't; he just blamed himself.

'We're not far from the station,' I said. 'Shall we take a chance?'

It was a pretty desperate chance, for Sandorski's description as well as mine would now be known. I went first, leaving the general and Lex in the shadow behind the parcels office. If I were arrested, there was still hope that they might get through and do our business at 26, Fulham Park Avenue.

There were no police in the booking office or on the platform. Though we could never be sure of it, we were always a few minutes ahead of the pursuit. Organization takes time and there aren't enough police. I expect some overworked bobby was already on his way to the station – but with instructions to check up on car parks as he went.

The ticket window was open, so there was a train due. I borrowed Lex's hat, glasses and overcoat, made my height as small as I could, and bought three tickets to London. I hoped that from inside the ticket office I looked the inoffensive citizen I felt, and wholly out of the murderous, car-wrecking character that had been forced on me.

As we crossed the bridge over the lines, a train for London came in from the west. There was another, apparently just about to start, going to Southampton. This was a gift, and singly and unobtrusively we entered it. That, we reckoned, would waste some more of the Wiltshire Constabulary's time.

The cross-country train rumbled down to the coast

untroubled, its few passengers gay or snoring. We had a compartment to ourselves. Lex, once more wrapped in his overcoat, dozed. Sandorski and I kept a careful lookout as the train stopped at the dim-lit country stations. No officials showed any curiosity about us. There was nothing we could have done if they had.

We were under no illusions. The police would surely have taken an interest in three tickets to London, booked just at the critical time, and three vaguely seen men, two of whom were of the right build. When they hadn't found us on the London train, it seemed likely that they would put a routine check on Southampton station. If we weren't there either, then we must be still in Salisbury.

And so Sandorski took another of his cavalry decisions. When the train stopped about a third of a mile outside Southampton Central, he gave a quick look up and down the line, and ordered us out.

As soon as I had lowered Lex to the ground, I felt that Sandorski had merely multiplied our chances of being caught. But he did nothing by halves. He dived between the wheels and lay flat on the permanent way, and we had to follow him. It was so swift and sensible, provided you could forget – as I could not – the chance of the train starting while one of us was wriggling over the rails.

The train pulled out over our heads, leaving Sandorski sputtering with indignant rage and all the monosyllables that his governess had taught him. He had been a little close to the outflow of the lavatory.

It wasn't a promising stretch of line. On both sides of it were fences, and beyond them wide deserts of waste ground. The only cover was a line of coal trucks in a siding. A mile away were the flood-lit funnels of the liners. I had a lovely daydream of being on board with Cecily and the children. It was a depressing spot, that blank bit of railway.

'You've done it this time,' I said. 'Easier to make New York than London.'

'We'll take a boat train. Why not?' he answered cheerfully.

'Because there aren't any at this time of night.'

'Well, what's wrong with that?' He patted the truck against which we were leaning. 'It must go somewhere some time.'

'But we don't know where, and Lex would be frozen to death.'

'Then Colonel, my lad, we'll stop a train!'

'How?'

'Red light. Or do they use green lights in England? Hell! Drive on the left of the road, don't you?'

'Suppose there's an accident?'

'Nonsense! Why should there be? Eh, Lex?'

'Accident to other people, not so?' asked Lex hopefully.

'You'll be in it too, my boy,' said Sandorski. 'Got a bit of red paper, Colonel?'

'Is it Christmas?'

'Infantryman – ha? No hole in the ground – no morale, ha? Where's that torch of yours?'

I stopped sulking and began to think. If he stopped a train there would be a determined search for the culprit, and the police might put two and two together.

'You always do the right thing,' I said, 'and then go plumb crazy when it works. Look here, if we went to Southampton by train, that's the only train we could have taken. Right! We weren't on it, so the cops go home to bed. If we're cautious we can use the station.'

The line was open and bare of possible cover. There was little chance of avoiding any railwaymen who might choose to walk along it at the same time as ourselves, or of bluffing them into believing that we had a right to be where we were. Assuming that the police had been chatting with stationmaster and staff, anyone answering the descriptions of Sandorski and myself would be under lively suspicion. No, it was absolutely essential to reach the station unnoticed. If we could, and if we found a place to wait for a London train, we should be clear of pursuit at last.

I went up the line to explore, leaving Lex and the general under cover of the coal trucks. My excuse was that I knew more of my own railways than Sandorski; but in fact I felt that his mood was too inspired for him to be let loose. Left to himself, he might easily have walked into the stationmaster's office and ordered a special train. I don't say he wouldn't have got it, but at this crisis of our fortunes I was all for a hole-in-the-ground policy.

Quarter of a mile up the line was a signal box blazing

with light, and beyond that the white gleam of the station and the dots of red and emerald on the tracks. I trotted from sleeper to sleeper, ready to drop flat at any moment, until I was under the wall of the box. That was the end of the advance. I might perhaps have tried to stalk the station if I had had only myself to consider, but there was no hope of getting the lumbering, overcoated Lex past the box and all the lights, and onto the bare platform, without some official shouting at us.

Even so I was confident that on a dark night, with all industry and transport – outside the station, that is – tucked up in bed or represented only by sleepy watch-men, it would be easy enough to find another route and to remain invisible. The little gods of luck, however – whom I may have offended by ascribing too much of our success to good management – were determined to show me to whom the gratitude was really due.

I went back down the line and started to climb the fence into the waste ground between railway and docks. The fence was only of split paling, but I got my trousers caught on the points. While I was trying to extricate myself a locomotive passed, clanking light-heartedly home. The driver shouted something, and the fireman heaved a lump of coal – more, I think, by way of a cheerfully disapproving gesture than with any intent of hitting the target; indeed, he might have tried for a month of journeys to score a bull and failed. The lump caught me on the back of the neck. The seat of my pants and the paling were smartly separated. Until I picked myself up I thought it was the locomotive itself which had hit me.

After crossing the waste ground and another fence I came out on to a road. It passed over the railway by a bridge, on each side of which were the approaches to the up and down platforms, spacious, well-lit and empty but for a solitary taxi. There were two massive cops outside the entrance to the up booking-office; the solidity of their overcoats made them look like a sculptor's functional decoration for the concrete buildings. While I watched them, they moved off. To us it didn't much matter whether they stayed or not. The railway men, mildly busy on the platforms, had certainly been warned to keep an eye open for fugitive murderers.

I leaned over the parapet of the bridge. The tracks and the roofs over the platforms were immediately below me. The roofs were accessible, easily accessible, and couldn't be seen from ground level. Was there any hope of a route and a refuge at the end of it? I saw several fantastic answers, and one that might be practical. In a bay alongside the down platform was a big empty restaurant car. If we could reach it, we could wait as long as we liked behind it or under it. The back of the car was close up against the wall of the station buildings, and in deep shadow.

Before I committed Lex and Sandorski, I decided to reconnoitre the route. The road appeared to be empty. I climbed on to the parapet and let myself silently down to the roof of the platform, which was only some six feet below. I had just started to crawl cautiously along the roof when a voice from the parapet called:

"Ere you! Wotcher doin' of?'

I shall never know how he managed to interrupt me. I think he must have been riding a bicycle without a light, or else had been watching me for some time from the shadows, as fascinated as any curious dog.

What to do? Take him into my confidence? Bluff? Climb back to the road and knock him out? I remember that all these alternatives went through my head, but I cannot have had time to formulate even mental words. How is it possible to think, I wonder, without the use of at least a few key-words in the brain? And yet, in an emergency, it is.

'Only getting a spot of free travel, mate,' I said.

'Doin' the railway company, eh?' he asked with an aggressive sense of duty.

'It ain't the company any longer,' I replied indignantly. 'It's the state.'

He thought that over.

'Ah, so it is,' he said. 'Well, good night!'

He removed his head and vanished as silently as he had appeared.

After all this interference by the citizenry, my nerves were shattered. I crawled along that roof, trying hard to persuade myself that it was safer than any other place I had been in for the last six hours – which, oddly enough, and at a distance of twenty feet from the bridge, was true.

When I came abreast of the rear end of the restaurant car, I saw that there would be no difficulty in dropping on to its roof, so long as feet didn't slip on its sloping edge. There was a risk, of course, that the lower half of anyone walking along the top of the car would be noticed from the platform, but it had to be taken.

I returned to the bridge, crossed the road and the fence beyond, and disappeared into the waste ground. Lex and Sandorski were waiting where I had left them in the darkness of the coal trucks. The general didn't much care for my route when I explained it, and asked whether I thought that Lex was a bloody circus performer. Lex, however, had cheered up a little. He insisted that if all he had to do was drop, the law of gravity would take care of him. It certainly would. What worried us was where he would land and how much noise he would make.

We passed Lex over the fence and made a wide circuit away from the railway so that our clumsy progress wouldn't be heard by anyone on the line. That journey was a violent strain on patience. The darkness was absolute – probably because there were so many lights in the distance to catch our eyes – and the surface was abominable. Holes, bricks, strands of wire, rusty cans and drums, all camouflaged by tall dead weeds, tripped us while we supported the stumbling Lex. It seemed all of a mile before we came to the road.

I went first to show them where to cross the parapet of

the bridge. A minute afterwards Lex sprawled over the edge into sight, with the general hanging on to his hands. I grabbed and landed him, and Sandorski followed. Once Lex had got his breath back, it seemed the right moment to stimulate him; so we had a stiff tot of rum all round.

Our crawl in single file along the roof was easy enough. We halted above the black whale-back of the restaurant car. I asked Lex if he thought that – with help – he could drop to it and keep his footing, and then quickly climb down to the couplings by the rungs at the rear of the car.

The rum worked.

'I have militär training,' he said proudly.

We couldn't let him make an enthusiastic job of it then and there, because we did not know what was going on beneath us. The platform might be empty, or there might be a whole group of railwaymen discussing the next day's football. I leaned over the edge of the concrete while Sandorski sat on my legs. With the top half of my body upside down, I surveyed the station. On our own platform no one was in sight; on the far platform there was some activity around the baggage office – not very strenuous, but sufficient to keep eyes from straying where they had no business.

'All clear for you, General,' I reported, wriggling back to the horizontal.

He dropped on to the roof of the car and was off it again with first bounce. He could now keep watch on the platforms for us, and signal to me from the narrow space between the back of the car and the buffers at the end of the bay.

When he beckoned, I too dropped and told Lex to follow. Strength or nerve failed him at the last moment, and he stuck with his chest on the edge of the concrete and his legs kicking wildly in air – just where I couldn't grab them without risk of falling off the top of the car myself. At that moment a porter chose to walk, whistling, round the corner of the station buildings. I caught Lex's legs as they lashed back, and prayed that he wouldn't let go his hold on the roof and that the porter wouldn't look up. For long seconds we formed a leaning, living bridge between restaurant car and roof until it was safe for me to whisper to him what to do and where to put his feet.

We dived under the van with, at last, no interested public but the station cat. She seemed to think that she could learn a thing or two from our movements, or perhaps considered us as promising kittens, and was showing us how an experienced adult would have done the job. At any rate, she put up such a dance of misplaced enthusiasm between station roof and car and buffers that the porter at the far end of the platform was interested and came back and started to call for puss. Thank God cats don't bark!

We didn't have a long wait. The second train in was for London – one of those slow and weightily important trains, usually empty, which stop everywhere to pick up the mails. I poked up a very cautious head. The platform was sparsely populated by porters and post office employees, and there was no convenient crowd of passengers alighting or boarding the train; it couldn't have been worse. And then a light engine came along, banged into the restaurant car, was coupled on, and prepared to draw our cover from over our heads.

It was a moment of hopeless, helpless disappointment. We stood up in my lookout post – between the back of the dining-car and the buffers – and waited to be revealed in all our guilty nakedness to the shunter and assistant stationmaster as soon as the car drew out. I don't know who first saw the way of escape. Even Lex didn't miss it, for he was trying to scramble up before I shoved him from behind. On the far side of the bay was a ledge, hardly wide enough to be called a platform. We had only to walk along that, keeping pace with the car as it was pulled away, and nobody – provided neither driver nor fireman looked to their right – could see us.

It worked. We trotted along by the flank of that friendly restaurant car, and when we were clear of the bay we saw salvation. There was a goods train standing on the far side of the London train, which we couldn't get a glimpse of from where we had been. We had only to walk up the permanent way between the two trains and get in from the wrong side.

The doors were already shut, and the night mail might start at any moment. We were weary of precautions. We crossed the rails in a bunch. I don't know if anyone saw us. If he did, he must have been too tired to bother with trespassing passengers. Once between the two trains, the rest was simple. We settled Lex in a steaming hot empty compartment, put his overcoat over his head, and went into another ourselves to breathe freely. Two minutes later the train left.

'Now,' said Sandorski, 'where's that needle and thread!'

Lex by this time had complete trust in us, and was convinced that the life we had led him for the last twenty-four hours was all for his own good. Every one of our actions was consistent with a desperate attempt to pass him through a cordon of police and private enemies, and deliver him to Heyne-Hassingham. Of course – for that was just what we were trying to do. He no longer worried about his brief-case; in any case, he could be sure it hadn't been tampered with, since it had not gone up in a burst of flame.

Sandorski undid our precious brown paper parcel. The bottom of the brief-case, relieved of string, gaped. The stuffing of paper fell out.

'Can you ever make a job of it?' I asked.

'Must,' he answered. 'And I made my own shoes in prison camp. How long have I got?'

'Well, expresses take an hour and a half. We can safely add another hour for this train.'

I think I never admired him so much as during that journey. I had no idea that he could be so meticulous. Every stitch that I had cut was lifted out, and with infinite care he drove his needle through the same holes. First he sewed the cardboard roll back to the inner side of the bag, leaving slack the wire between the latch and the incendiary, so that even when the device was set it wouldn't go off. Then he put back the loose paper and stitched up the seam. The only thing he could not restore exactly as we found it was the sealed tape that ran the length of the roll and round the two ends. We stuck the cut edges of the tape to the cardboard, and hoped that Heyne-Hassingham, in his general state of agitation, wouldn't notice. The trigger wire of the incendiary still ran through the tape, so it was pretty certain he would cut, withdraw his documents and never look at roll or tape again.

Lex had not seen his brief-case at all since he packed. He had only seen the parcel, which was beginning to look disreputable. We brushed the drying mud from our clothes, remixed it and smeared it artistically here and there over the case to hide the newness of the thread. Then we wrapped up the parcel again and soaked the lower end in mud and water. When Lex handled it, the paper would certainly disintegrate and the dirt of the case would need no explanation.

While Sandorski was working on his long task I stood in the corridor, in case Lex should take it into his head to get up and disturb us. He didn't. He was only too thankful to be able to lie down in peace. I visited him occasionally. At Winchester he stared into the night and burbled something about King Alfred and Law. He was a well-read blighter.

After Basingstoke, where the line from Salisbury joined that from Southampton, we were – potentially, at any rate – in danger again. I felt it was slight. To the police, after checking the likely trains, it must appear that we were still in or around Salisbury. It was certain, however, that there would be a routine control at Waterloo. I wanted to leave the train at one of the suburban stations, but Sandorski wouldn't have it; he feared that, as the only passengers getting out, we should attract attention.

Three-quarters of our job, he said, was now done. Lex had his brief-case and papers seemingly intact, and so long as he kept away from us there was nothing to prevent him leaving the terminus and taking a taxi to 26, Fulham Park Avenue. The police had no description of him. What happened to us didn't matter much, but it would be more comfortable and discreet to be arrested in Fulham Park Avenue than elsewhere.

We woke up Lex, who was feeling brighter, and Sandorski gave him his instructions in rapid German, which he translated to me afterwards. Early in the morning Lex was to telephone Heyne-Hassingham and tell him that he had escaped during some trouble or other at the landing of the plane, which looked like an attempt to kidnap him. He had got clear, had spent the day in a village, lying low and finding out where he was, and had then taken a late train to London. He was to obey his instructions to hand over his brief-case to Heyne-Hassingham in person, and he was to ask Heyne-Hassingham to come to London to receive it. He was not to talk of his adventures or to mention his address on the telephone, but simply to say he was where he had been told to go in any emergency.

The train pulled in to Waterloo. We pushed Lex out on to the platform and said good-bye. Then we hid under the seats, feeling unnecessarily cowardly. It was wiser, however, to reach Sandorski's friend, Roland, if we could, without a chance of police or Hiart or Hiart's agents intervening.

We stayed under the seats for about twenty minutes while the train was trundled out, and banged back and forth in the yards. It stopped at one or two unpromising places, where we were in a blaze of lights and suspended above south London on arches. We didn't like the look of them and remained. Then an army of cleaners swarmed over our train.

'Quick! Sleep!' Sandorski ordered.

He pulled the cork out of the rum and dropped the bottle on the floor. We lay back snoring. A fearsome female, all dirt, muscles and overalls, poked us with the end of her broom.

''Ere!' she exclaimed. 'Look what 'appened to the drop you were tykin' 'ome for muvver!'

'Where are we?' I murmured, with a stage hiccup.

'On the bleedin' British Rylewyes,' she said. 'And don't think because you own 'em you can myke 'em a bleedin' 'otel.'

We staggered to our feet, and I'm damned if Sandorski didn't try to kiss her. That got him altogether too

137

much goodwill, and if some kind of official hadn't come along I doubt if anything would have saved him from a fate worse than death right here in the compartment. The official was sternly humorous. He was evidently quite accustomed to finding bits of rubbish like ourselves routed out by cleaners from late trains. He collected our tickets, escorted us firmly to a gate, and left us free in London.

It was dark and cold and raining. Somewhere near Vauxhall Bridge we found a taxi, and told the driver to take us to Fulham Park Avenue and stop at the corner. He seemed to know what corner, so I left it at that. The empty, mournful streets were unending. I hoped the children were asleep. I knew Cecily wouldn't be.

'Now look here, Colonel, my lad! said Sandorski. 'You leave it all to me. Not a word about Riemann! You've just been helping me. I picked you up on your shoot. Thought you were obviously a useful chap. We don't know anything about the corpse in the car. Leave him out altogether. Tell the rest as it happened.'

No. 26 was an unassuming block of flats, three stories high. No lifts. No porter. Just the place for quiet comings and goings with no questions asked. As we hesitated invitingly in front of the closed door, I thought I saw somebody in the wet and gleaming patch of darkness across the road flash a torch quickly towards the roof of No. 26. Sandorski waited, confident in his friend's arrangements.

The front door opened quietly.

'Well, Peter,' whispered a voice. 'Got here after all, by Jove!'

'Anyone come in?' Sandorski asked.

'Yes. He's up there.'

'With parcel?'

'With parcel.'

'Then you won't have anything to do till morning. Take us where we can talk.'

'Don't mind if I do,' said the voice. 'It's cold up there on the water tank.'

Two men came out of the house and closed the door behind them. We all walked away together. The chap next to Sandorski was slim and fair. In dark sweater and wind-breaker, with a disreputable hat, he looked much like my idea of an enterprising burglar. His walk and bearing, however, were free and casual. The man at my side – and very close to my side he was – had a conventional hat and overcoat. His face was heavy but intelligent – and, at the moment, remarkably expressionless. We walked to the police car, which was parked some distance away, in an embarrassing silence. When we got there, my companion asked me if I were Colonel Taine.

'Mr Taine,' I corrected him.

'I have a warrant for your arrest on a charge of murder of a person unknown ...' and he gave me the details and the usual caution.

I don't mind saying that his neutral, even kindly voice

moved me to a sheer panic such as I've never felt in all my life.

'You can take down any damn thing you please in evidence against us,' interrupted Sandorski cheerfully. 'Got a sharp pencil – ha?'

'Peter,' the other man said to him with the utmost seriousness, 'you do understand that if you have broken the law I can't help you, don't you?'

'Haven't even hit a policeman,' Sandorski replied. 'Get on with it! Where can we talk?'

'Why not my flat – if you've no objection, Inspector?'

I think that perhaps this friend of Sandorski's – and now of mine – would prefer me not to give his name and address. So I will continue to call him Roland, and merely say that his flat was warm and welcome – especially when he had produced something to eat from the ice-box. The policeman was Inspector Haldon of Scotland Yard's Special Branch.

Sandorski told our story. He said that he had come to England on information received, and left it at that. He had run into me when exploring the shoot, and I had agreed to help him. We had found the beacons and intercepted the plane, and we knew nothing at all about the body in the car. Then he told them of the international connections of the People's Union, and that it was Robert Heyne-Hassingham and Hiart who had organized the illicit landing.

Roland was at first inclined to think that Sandorski was

romanticizing. He said that nobody could be such a fool as to take the People's Union seriously, not even its founder; and he was horrified at the suggestion that Hiart, who was almost a colleague of his, could be implicated.

He appealed to Inspector Haldon, who grinned in answer.

'I must admit, sir,' he said, 'that Colonel Hiart – well, it *has* been suggested that he was rather too thick with some of his opposite numbers abroad. We keep an open mind, of course, but—'

'Good God, Haldon!' Roland exclaimed, really shocked. 'Do you watch me, too?'

'Fatherly, sir, fatherly,' said the inspector. 'Now, General, I understand that you telephoned Mr Roland last night to wire Flat 9 for sound in order that you could prove your innocence and Mr Taines. What are we going to hear?'

'You are going to hear that courier speak to Heyne-Hassingham, and I hope you're going to hear him hand over the documents.'

Then Sandorski told him what the documents were.

'Now you see why we ran for it – ha? If Hiart had got his hands on that brief-case, soon have gone up in smoke, wouldn't it? And if the police had it first, he'd have sworn the papers were forged by a mad Pole. Crazy general. Brains removed for experiment in prison camp. Lands planes. Burns cars. And the passenger, so that he can't talk – ha? I'd have had a hard time proving it wasn't so. I may have, still. I'm not sure Heyne-Hassingham will come. He might send Hiart.'

'He won't do that,' said Roland. 'Hiart's in hospital.'

'Pink shot him?'

'Good lord, Peter, this is England! He fractured his skull when his car tipped over.'

'Now this is all very well, sir,' said the inspector genially. 'But what we want to know is if General Sandorski can throw any light at all on that burned body.'

'I? Didn't know a thing about it till the cops called on Taine.'

'Or you, Mr Taine?'

'No,' I said, 'no ... no.'

'Would it surprise you to know that the man had been dead some weeks before he was burned?'

'It would delight me,' said Sandorski. 'Here's my passport! You can see I wasn't in England.'

'And Mr Taine?'

'It's only a week since I met the general,' I replied, as if that fixed it.

Well, of course, it did. My life was an open book. Haldon must have been wholly content that I had no conceivable motive to go around murdering strangers until Sandorski turned up.

'By the way,' the inspector asked, 'what did you do with Mr Bear's limousine? We'd better get hold of that before there's any trouble about it.'

'Left it at Salisbury.'

'Then you did come by train?'

'Sure we did,' said Sandorski. 'Why not? Give your chaps a lecture any time you like, Inspector. Hints and Tips on Train Control.'

Roland let us doss down in his flat, while he and Haldon returned to duty at 26, Fulham Park Avenue. The inspector didn't exactly put us on parole, but he did warn us that he had a man outside, and that we couldn't avoid publicity and a magistrate's court if we tried to escape. As soon as they had gone, I tried to call Cecily. Only after sweating with fury did I remember that twelve hours before Sandorski had cut the line.

I thought that our excitement and exhaustion were too insistent for sleep, but some time after dawn we must both have dozed off, for we were awakened by Roland returning with the news that it was eleven o'clock and that he had a transcript of the telephone conversation between Lex and Heyne-Hassingham.

Lex had done very well. He had a fine Central European obstinacy. The butler tried to put him off. He kept on ringing, and attracted the private secretary. At last he got on to the great leader himself. Heyne-Hassingham had been very cagey and incredulous, but Lex started to give him the exact details of when he had been sent and by whom. Then Heyne-Hassingham exploded:

'Good God, Riemann!'

Roland looked at us for an explanation, but both Sandorski and I were blank – I fear, suspiciously blank. Of course Heyne-Hassingham had believed the corpse in the car to be Lex, and he now saw that it must be the vanished Riemann.

After that he wanted Lex to come down to his house in Dorset, but Lex wasn't having any. He thought London was much safer – and I'm not surprised. So, on second thoughts, did Heyne-Hassingham. He had promised to drive up to town immediately.

Roland packed us into the back of his car, with a very formidable character sitting between us. A former commando sergeant-major, I should think. He looked too lawless for any policeman. It was clear that we were by no means trusted yet.

'Does Heyne-Hassingham know whose body that was in the car?' asked Roland, as soon as he had cleared Trafalgar Square and was driving evenly westwards along the Mall.

'He does,' the general answered. 'What was the name he exclaimed when Lex called him up? Something like Riemann, wasn't it?'

'He knows who killed him, too?'

'No. Thinks I did. He'll tell you so.'

'How good is your alibi really?' Roland asked, staring straight ahead of him into the traffic.

'Perfect. I was in Vienna up to last week.'

'Day and night, Peter?'

'Nearly. I'd have needed a damn fast plane if I did it – and *you* ought to know my funds don't run to that.'

Before we turned into Fulham Park Avenue we were stopped by one of Haldon's men, who told us that half an hour after the conversation between Lex and Heyne-Hassingham two chaps had turned up in the street and were hanging about; one of them was known to be the Fulham secretary of the People's Union. It was a sure bet that they were going to report to the revered leader, when his car stopped at the corner, whether anyone suspicious had gone into No. 26.

That didn't bother Roland. I gathered that the Metropolitan Police by no means always used the front door of a house that interested them. At No. 38 there was a friendly porter, bursting with importance and carefully looking the other way when we passed him. From a skylight in his building we gained access to the roofs of the long, narrow block, and walked along the leads, between the sloping slates and the parapet, to No. 26. We had to climb the party walls, with their projecting chimney stacks, but were hidden from Fulham Park Avenue itself by the gables. We were, of course, in full view of windows of the opposite block, beyond the yards and gardens. Londoners, however, have a remarkable lack of curiosity.

Haldon and a police stenographer were squatting in the shelter of a water tank. We waited with them for some ninety minutes of cold politeness. Then the front-door bell of Flat 9 spat a startling ring at us from the receiver, and we settled down to listen.

The door opened and shut. Lex took control of the

interview from the start, for he insisted solidly upon Heyne-Hassingham proving his identity. When his legal mind was satisfied, and Heyne-Hassingham – to judge by his voice – dancing with impatience, Lex said:

'Here is vot I bring for you! I push – so! – and we may open. If I not push, all burn!'

'Very ingenious,' agreed Heyne-Hassingham coldly and hurriedly.

He was a frightened man. His hoarse tone was enough for Haldon to give me a confident wink. It was the first friendly gesture that the inspector had permitted himself.

They must have been very close to the microphone, for we actually heard the key turn in the lock of the brief-case, and then a rustle of papers, overwhelmingly loud, as Heyne-Hassingham withdrew the roll of documents and glanced at the contents.

He pulled himself together and thanked Lex for his de-voted service in words that would better have fitted the Archbishop of Canterbury than a damned idealistic crook of a politician.

'I did little,' Lex answered. 'But soch gallantry, soch bravery I have seen! I vant you now to hear—'

'I will, my dear chap, I will indeed,' Heyne-Hassingham interrupted. 'But later, if you don't mind. I must get you out of England at once. You'll have your orders in an hour or two. Understood?'

Haldon jumped for the skylight of No. 26, intending to

pick up Heyne-Hassingham outside the door of the flat before he could get rid of his papers.

'Don't touch Lex!' Sandorski shouted. 'And don't take Heyne-Hassingham past the windows. It's a gift!'

Roland saw what he meant at once. If Lex stayed in the flat and knew nothing of Heyne-Hassingham's arrest, and if Sandorski then smuggled him abroad, it would be proved up to the hilt the general was indeed Heyne-Hassingham's trusted agent, and, for a few days at any rate, all Lex's contacts would be wide open to inspection.

Heyne-Hassingham's head and shoulders appeared at the skylight, with Haldon a close two rungs of the ladder below him. For a moment the great leader looked his part. Worry and terror and self-control had given him the ascetic face of a saint.

He took two fairly confident steps towards the water tank. Then he saw me, knew that he was trapped, and had, I suppose, no thought but how to get rid of his papers. He lost his nerve, jumped the low party wall on to the leads of the next house and bolted. It wasn't as crazy an act as it seemed. If he could get a lead of a few seconds and drop that roll of documents down a smoking chimney pot, he could afford to stand on his dignity afterwards.

Sandorski went away after him well ahead of the rest of us. His featherweight build was just right for this gymnasium stuff; he could hop over the slates like a London sparrow. Heyne-Hassingham managed to keep away from him for the length of half a dozen houses, and then, when the general was nearly on him, jumped on to the parapet overlooking Fulham Park Avenue. I don't know what he meant to do. His position was by no means desperate enough for suicide. But he was unbalanced in more senses than one, and it was Sandorski's grab for him that was decisive. I was the only person who saw what happened. Sandorski was, perhaps, a little clumsy. It was as well, for I doubt if Haldon could ever have got a conviction for high treason against a competent defence.

The punishment, however, was correct. Heyne-Hassingham fell on the area railings beneath, and a spike took him under the chin. When we got down to the street we couldn't see much of his sprawling body, but his head looked at us as if from the top of Temple Bar. A mean and suburban Temple Bar – that was about what Heyne-Hassingham was worth.

At Scotland Yard Haldon took me first, and alone. I didn't have any difficulty. I told the whole truth and nothing but the truth, but I started it with the appearance of Sandorski on my shoot. I had merely to appear a bit of a romantic fool, showing myself far too easily convinced by Sandorski's story.

'Somewhat irresponsible for a married man with children, isn't it?' asked Haldon.

'Oh, well,' I replied weakly, 'one wants to escape from time to time, you know.'

'You'd better tell that to Mrs Taine,' he said, with a dryness that suggested he wasn't wholly satisfied.

He pressed a bell on his desk. There was a moment of awkward silence. Then the door opened, and in came Cecily.

Damn Haldon! I couldn't help it. I seemed to have been away from her for a year.

'Who's looking after the children?' I asked.

'I told the police they had to come with me,' she said. 'There's a sergeant out there, playing with them. They wanted to see how handcuffs worked.'

She stifled a sob and looked at us both, very still but not white. She forced herself to appear natural and proud. I don't know how she did it.

'Mrs Taine,' said Haldon. 'There's just one point I want cleared up. You stated to the Dorset police that you were absolutely certain that no one had ever been hidden in your house. Would you care to amend that?'

'No,' she answered. 'No one was ever hidden in my house.'

I could have believed her myself. I said:

'It's all right, darling. Tell him the truth.'

'That's very wrong of you, Inspector,' she complained hotly. 'How was I to know? Of course there were two of them in the roof, General Sandorski and a man they called Lex.'

'I see,' he answered with a heavy neutrality. 'Mrs Taine, when did you first know that your husband was engaged in these activities?'

That was a vilely clever question. I stayed frozen, for

Haldon was watching both our faces. If she answered that she had known for three weeks, I was done.

'What activities?' she asked.

'Assisting the police.'

'Oh, when he brought General Sandorski home the first time,' she replied, straight off the bat.

'Thank you, Mrs Taine. I should say perhaps that my report from the Dorset police' – was there a shade of irony in his voice? – 'states that you gave an impression of absolute honesty and innocence.'

'Didn't I?' I asked.

'You were rather too pleased with your acting, Mr Taine;' he replied, and added mysteriously: 'It's a fault that Mr Roland will doubtless take in hand. We don't want to lose people like you, you know.'

He let Cecily go, telling her that he would only detain me another minute. Then he joined me on the public side of his desk and produced a decanter of whisky.

'We're allowed a good deal of liberty at the Special Branch,' he said.

I answered that I had noticed it. He had tidied up Fulham Park Avenue with remarkable speed.

'Heyne-Hassingham was a prominent man,' he went on, 'and I think I shall be permitted to make the inquest as uncomplicated as possible. No Lex. No Sandorski. Just a combination of a routine police enquiry and overwork. That will give us time to throw the net a little wider. But there is just one thing bothering me, and I daren't leave it hanging about unsolved in the background. That corpse in the car. If you can, let me have a statement for the files – completely off the record, as a little bit of fiction, perhaps – just so that I know what happened.'

THE END